NOBODY
LIVES FOREVER

JAMES BOND

NOBODY LIVES FOREVER

JOHN GARDNER

PEGASUS BOOKS
NEW YORK

NOBODY LIVES FOREVER

Pegasus Books LLC
80 Broad Street, 5th Floor
New York, NY 10004

Library of Congress Cataloging-in-Publication Data is available.

ISBN: 978-1-60598-340-0

10 9 8 7 6 5 4 3 2 1

Printed in the United States of America
Distributed by W. W. Norton & Company, Inc.
www.pegasusbooks.us

For
Peter & Peg
With Affection

CONTENTS

NOBODY
LIVES FOREVER

— 1 —
No Way to
Start a Vacation

JAMES BOND SIGNALED LATE, braked more violently than a Bentley driving instructor would have
liked, and slewed the big car off the E5 motorway and
onto the last exit road just north of Brussels.

It was merely a precaution. If he was going to
reach Strasbourg before midnight it would have
made more sense to carry on, follow the ring road
around Brussels, then keep going south on the
Belgian N4. Yet even on holiday, Bond knew that it
was only prudent to remain alert. The small detour
across country would quickly establish whether anyone was on his tail, and he would pick up the E40 in
about an hour or so.

Lately there had been a directive to all officers of
the Service advising "constant vigilance, even when

11

off duty, and particularly when on leave and out of the country."

He had taken the morning ferry to Ostend, and there had been over an hour's delay. About halfway into the crossing the ship had stopped, a boat was lowered, and they began to move—in a wide searching circle. After some forty minutes the boat returned and a helicopter appeared overhead as they set sail again. A little later the news spread throughout the ship. Two men overboard, and lost, it seemed. "Couple of young passengers skylarking," said the barman. "Skylarked once too often. Probably cut to shreds by the screws."

Eventually they arrived and, once through customs, Bond pulled into a side street, operated the secret compartment in the dashboard of the Bentley Mulsanne Turbo, checked that his 9mm ASP automatic was intact, with the spare ammunition clips, and took out the small concealable operations baton, which lay heavy in its soft leather holster.

Unobserved, he closed the compartment, loosened his belt and threaded the holster into place so that the weapon hung at his right hip. The baton was an effective piece of hardware: a black rod, no more than six inches long. When used by a trained man it could be lethal.

Shifting in the driving seat now, Bond felt the hard metal dig comfortably into his hip. He slowed the car to a crawl of 40 kph, scanning the mirrors,

12

taking corners and bends and automatically slowing again once on the far side. Within half an hour he was certain that he was not being followed.

Even with the memo in mind, he reflected that he was being more careful than usual. A sixth sense of danger? Or, possibly, M's remark a couple of days ago?

"You couldn't have chosen a more awkward time to be away, 007," his Chief had grumbled, typically begrudging when it came to matters of leave.

"It's only my entitlement, sir. You agreed I could take my month now. Don't forget, I had to postpone it earlier in the year."

M grunted.

"Moneypenny's going to be away as well. Off gallivanting all over Europe. You're not. . . ?"

"Accompanying Miss Moneypenny? No, sir."

"Off to Jamaica or one of your usual Caribbean haunts, I suppose?" M frowned.

"No, sir. Rome first. Then a few days on the Riviera dei Fiori before driving across to Austria—to pick up May. I just hope my housekeeper'll be fit enough to be brought back to London by then."

"Yes . . . Yes." M was not, however, appeased. "Well, leave your full itinerary with the Chief of Staff. Never know when we're going to need you."

"Already done, sir."

"Well, take care, 007. Take particular care. The Continent's a hotbed of villainy these days, and you can never be too careful." There was a sharp, steely look in his eyes—as though he knew something that was being hidden from Bond.

As Bond left M's office, the old man had the grace to say he hoped there would be good news about May.

At the moment, May, Bond's devoted old Scottish housekeeper, appeared to be the only worry on an otherwise cloudless horizon.

During the winter she had suffered two severe attacks of bronchitis and seemed to be physically deteriorating. She had been with Bond more years than either cared to remember. In fact, apart from the Service, she was the one constant in his not uneventful life.

After the second bronchial attack, he had insisted on a thorough checkup by a Service-retained doctor with a Harley Street practice, and though May had resisted—insisting she was "tough as an auld game bird, and no yet fit for the pot"—Bond had taken her personally to the doctor's consulting rooms.

There had followed an agonizing week, with May being passed from specialist to specialist, complaining all the way. But the tests had proved undeniably positive. The left lung was badly damaged, and there was a distinct possibility that the disease that now showed itself might spread. Unless the lung was removed immediately—followed by a good three

14

months of enforced rest and care for the patient—
May was unlikely to see her next birthday.

The operation was carried out by the most skillful
surgeon Bond's money could provide, and once she
was well enough, May had been packed off to one of
the best convalescence clinics in the world, the Klinik
Mozart, in the mountains south of Salzburg, where,
they informed Bond when he regularly telephoned,
she was making amazing progress.

He had even spoken to her personally the evening
before, and he now smiled to himself at the tone of
her voice, and the somewhat depreciating way she
had spoken of the Klinik. She was, no doubt, re-
organizing its staff and calling down the wrath of her
Glen Orchy ancestors on everyone from maids to
chefs.

"They dinna know how to cook yon decent wee
bite here, Mr. James, that's the truth of it; and the
maids canna make a bed for twopence. I'd no employ
any the one of them—and you paying all this money
for me to be here. Yon's a downright waste, Mr.
James. A *crinimal* waste." May had never been able to
get her tongue round the word "criminal."

He checked the fuel, deciding it would be best to
get the tank filled before the long drive that lay ahead
on the E40. Having established there was nobody on
his tail, he now concentrated on looking for a garage.
It was after seven in the evening, and there was little

15

traffic about. He drove through two small villages, and saw the signs indicating proximity to the motorway; then, on a straight, empty stretch of road, he spotted the garish signs of a small filling station.

It appeared to be deserted, though the door to the tiny office had been left open and the two pumps were unattended. A notice in red warned that the pumps were *not* self-service, so he pulled the Mulsanne up to the "super" pump, switched off the engine and climbed out, stretching his muscles, almost immediately alert to the noises coming from behind the little glass and brick building. Growling, angry voices, and a thump, as though someone had collided with a car.

Bond operated the central locking device on the car and strode quickly to the corner of the building. Within seconds he was moving with real speed.

Behind the office lay a garage area, in front of which stood a white Alfa Romeo Sprint. Two young men were beside the bonnet, across which they held down a third person, a girl. The driver's door was open and a handbag lay on the ground, its zipper ripped open and contents scattered.

"Come on," one of the young men spoke in rough French. "Where is it? You must have some! Give." Like his companion, the thug was dressed in faded jeans and sneakers. Both men were short and broad-shouldered, with tanned muscular arms.

16

The girl protested, and the man who had spoken raised his hand to hit her across the face.

"Stop that!" Bond's voice cracked like a whip as he moved forward.

Both men looked up, startled. Then one of them smiled. "Two for the price of one," he said softly, grabbing the girl by the shoulder and throwing her away from the car, his partner standing over her as she sprawled on the ground.

The man who faced Bond now held a large wrench and obviously thought Bond was easy meat. His hair was tight and curly, and the surly young face already showed the scars of a street fighter. He came forward fast, in a half crouch, holding the wrench low. He moved like a large monkey, Bond thought, reaching for the baton on his right hip as the mugger sprang.

The baton, made by the same firm which developed the 9mm ASP pistol, looks harmless enough—six inches of nonslip rubber-coated metal. But, as he drew it from its holster, Bond flicked down hard with his right wrist. From the rubber-covered handle sprang a further, telescoped ten inches of toughened steel, which locked into place.

The sudden appearance of the weapon took the young thug off guard. His right arm was raised, clutching the wrench, and for a second he hesitated. Bond stepped quickly to his left and swung the baton.

17

There was an unpleasant cracking noise, followed by a yelp, as the baton connected with the attacker's forearm. He dropped the wrench and doubled up, holding his broken arm, cursing in violent French.

Again Bond moved, delivering a lighter tap, this time to the back of the neck. The mugger went onto his knees and then pitched forward, out for the count as, with a roar, Bond hurled himself at the second thug.

But the man had no stomach for a fight, turning and starting to run. Not fast enough, though, for the tip of the baton came down hard on his left shoulder, certainly breaking bones.

He gave a louder cry than his partner, then raised his hands and began to plead. But Bond was in no mood to be kind to a couple of young *voyous* who had preyed on a virtually helpless woman. He lunged forward, burying the baton's tip in the man's groin, eliciting a further screech of pain that was cut off by a smart blow to the left of the neck, neatly judged to bring unconsciousness and do little further damage.

Bond kicked the wrench out of the way and turned to give the girl assistance, but she was already gathering her things together by the car.

"You all right?" He walked toward her—taking in the long tangle of red hair, the tall, lithe body, oval face, large brown eyes and Italianate look.

"Yes. Thank you, yes."

She had no trace of accent, and, as he came closer,

18

he noted the Gucci loafers, the very long legs encased in tight Calvin Klein jeans, and the silk Hermes shirt.

"Lucky you came along when you did," she said. "You think we should call the police?"

She gave her head a little shake, stuck out her bottom lip, and blew the hair out of her eyes.

"I just wanted petrol." Bond looked at the Alfa Romeo. "What actually happened?"

"I suppose you might say that I caught them with their fingers in the till, and they didn't take kindly to that. The attendant's out cold in the office, by the way."

The thugs, posing as attendants, had apologized when she drove in, saying the pumps out front were not working: Could she take the car to the pump around the back? "I fell for it, and they dragged me out of the car."

Bond asked how she knew about the attendant.

"One of them asked the other if he'd be okay. He said the man would be out for an hour or so." Her voice betrayed no sign of tension, and as she smoothed the tangle of hair, her hands were steady. "If you want to be on your way, I can telephone the police. There's really no need for you to hang about, you know."

"Nor you," he smiled. "Those two'll also be asleep for some time. The name's Bond, by the way. James Bond."

"Sukie," she held out a hand, the palm dry and the grip firm. "Sukie Tempesta."

In the end, they both waited for the police, though it cost Bond over an hour and a half's delay. The pump attendant had been badly beaten and urgently required medical attention. Sukie did what she could for him, while Bond telephoned the police. Then, as they waited, he talked to the girl, dropping innocent questions designed to find out more about her, for the whole affair had begun to intrigue him, and he had the impression she was holding out on him. But, however cleverly he phrased the queries, Sukie managed to sidestep, giving him answers that told him nothing.

There was little to be gleaned from observation either. She was very self-possessed, with a businesslike manner, and could have been anything, from a lawyer to a high-class tart. She looked well-off, judging by her clothes and the jewelry she wore. Certainly an attractive young woman, all in all, with a low-pitched voice, precise economic movements, and a reserved manner that was possibly a touch diffident.

One thing Bond did discover, quickly, was that she spoke both English and French fluently, which pointed to both intelligence and a good education. As for the rest, he could not even discover her nationality, though the plates on the Sprint were—like her name—Italian.

Before the police arrived with a flurry of sirens, Bond went back to his car and stowed away the baton—an illegal weapon in any country. He submitted to an interrogation, at the end of which he was asked to sign a statement. Only then was he allowed to fill up the car and leave, with the proviso that he gave his likely addresses for the next few weeks, and his address and number in London.

Sukie Tempesta was still being questioned when he drove away, feeling strangely uneasy. He recalled the look in M's eyes, and began to wonder about the business on the ferry.

The incident at the petrol station led to yet another, which happened just after midnight, on the E25 between Metz and Strasbourg.

Bond had again filled the tank, and drunk some passable coffee at the frontier post, when crossing into France. Now the road was almost deserted, so he spotted the tail lights of the car ahead a good two miles before overtaking it.

Out of habit, his eyes flicked to the number plate. It was a big white BMW and the number registered in his mind, as did the international *D* that proclaimed its German origin.

After crossing the frontier, he had set the cruise control at 110 kph and sailed past the BMW, which appeared to be pottering along in the eighties.

A minute or so later, Bond became alert. The BMW had picked up speed, moving into the center lane, yet remaining close to him, the distance varying between a quarter of a mile and a few hundred yards.

He touched the brakes, taking out the cruise con-

21

trol, and accelerated. One hundred and thirty. One hundred and fifty. The BMW was still there.

Then, with about ten miles to run before reaching the outskirts of Strasbourg, he became aware of another set of headlights, directly behind him in the fast lane and coming up at speed.

He switched into the middle lane, eyes flicking between the road ahead and the mirror. The BMW had fallen back a little, and in seconds the oncoming lights grew, and the Bentley was rocked slightly as a little black car went past like a jet. It must have been touching 180 kph and, in his headlights, Bond could only get a glimpse of the plates splattered with mud. His main impression was that they were Swiss; he was almost certain that he had caught sight of the Ticino Canton shield to the right of the rear plate. There was not enough time for him to identify the make of the vehicle—just low, black and very fast.

The BMW remained in place for a few moments only, appearing to slow and lose ground. Then Bond saw the flash in his mirror: a brutal crimson ball erupting in the middle lane behind him. He felt the Bentley shudder as the shock waves hit and watched in the mirror as a series of violent flaming shapes appeared to dance across the motorway.

Bond increased pressure on the accelerator. Nothing would make him stop and become involved at this time of night, particularly on a lonely stretch of road. Within a few minutes he realized that he felt oddly shaken at the unexplained violence that appeared to have surrounded him during the day.

At one-eleven in the morning, the Bentley nudged its way into Strasbourg's Place Saint-Pierre-le-Jeune to stop outside the Hotel Sofitel. The night staff was deferential—"Oui, Monsieur Bond . . . Non, Monsieur Bond." But certainly they had his reservation. The car was unloaded, his baggage whipped away, and he personally took the Bentley to the hotel's private parking.

The suite proved to be almost too large for the overnight stay, and there was a large basket of fruit, compliments of the manager. Bond did not know whether to be impressed or to be on his guard. He had not stayed at the Sofitel for at least three years.

Opening the minibar, he mixed himself a martini—pleased the bar stocked Gordons and a decent vodka, though he had to make do with a simple Lillet vermouth instead of his preferred Kina. Taking the drink over to the bed, Bond selected one of his two briefcases, the one that contained the sophisticated scrambling equipment, which he attached to the phone before dialing Transworld Exports—the Service headquarters' cover—in London.

The duty officer listened patiently while Bond recounted the two incidents in some detail. The line was quickly closed, and Bond, tired after the long drive, took a quick shower, rang down for a call at eight in the morning and, naked, stretched out under the down cover.

Only then did Bond start to face up to the fact that he was more than a little edgy. He kept thinking of that strange look in M's eyes. Then he thought about the Ostend ferry and the two men overboard; the girl—Sukie—in distress at the filling station; and the deadly explosion on the road. It was too much to be mere coincidence, and a shadow of menace started to creep into his head.

— 2 —

The Poison Dwarf

BOND SWEATED THROUGH his morning exercise routine—the normal twenty slow pushups with their exquisite lingering strain; then the leg lifts, performed on the stomach; and lastly the twenty fast toe-touches.

Before going to the shower, he called room service and gave exact instructions for breakfast—two thick slices of whole-wheat bread, with their best butter and, if possible, Tiptree "Little Scarlet" jam and Cooper's Marmalade. Alas, monsieur, there was no Cooper, but they had Tiptree. It was unlikely they could supply De Bry coffee, so, after a question and answer routine, he settled for their special blend. While waiting for the tray to arrive, he took a very hot shower, followed by one with the water freezing cold.

He did not like change, being a man of habit, but

had recently altered his soap, shampoo and cologne to Dunhill Blend 30—deciding they held a more masculine tang—and now, after a vigorous toweling, he rubbed cologne into his body before slipping into his silk traveling "Happi-coat" to await breakfast, which came complete with all the local morning papers.

The BMW, or what small amount of debris was left, seemed to be spread across all the front pages, while the headlines proclaimed its destruction to be everything from an atrocious act of urban terrorism to the latest assassination in a criminal gang war that appeared to have been sweeping France over the last few weeks.

There was little detail, except for the police claim that there was only one victim—the driver—and that the car was registered in the name of Conrad Tempel, a German businessman from Freiburg. Herr Tempel was missing from his home, so they presumed he was mixed up in shreds among the pieces of blasted motor car.

While reading the story, Bond drank his two large cups of black coffee, without sugar, reflecting that he would skirt Freiburg later that day, after driving into Germany. He planned to cross the Swiss frontier later, at Basel, and, once in Switzerland, would make his way down to Lake Maggiore in the Ticino Canton, and spend a night in one of the small tourist villages on the Swiss side of the Lake. Tomorrow he could plan for a final long run into Italy—a lengthy sweat over the autostradas to Rome and a few days with the Service's Resident and his wife—Steve and Tabitha Quinn.

Today's drive would not be so taxing. He did not need to leave until noon, so had a little time to look around and relax, but first there was the most important ritual of the morning—the telephone call to the Klinik Mozart, near Salzburg, to inquire after May.

He dialed the French "out" code, 19, followed by the 61 that would take him into the Austrian system, then the number. Once the Klinik answered he asked to be put through to the Herr Direktor—Herr Doktor Kirchtum—who came on the line almost immediately.

"Good morning, Mr. Bond. You are in Belgium now, yes?"

Bond said no, he was in France, tomorrow Switzerland and Italy on the following day.

"You are burning a lot of the rubber, as they say." Kirchtum was a large man, and his voice was full of boom and resonance. At the Klinik he could be heard in a room long before he arrived. The nurses called him *das Nebelhorn*—"the Foghorn."

Bond asked after May.

"She still does well. Orders us around, which is a good sign of recovery." Kirchtum gave a guffaw of laughter. "I think the chef is about to cash in his index, as I believe you English say."

"Hand in his cards." Bond smiled to himself. The

Herr Doktor, he was sure, made very studied errors in colloquial English. He asked if there was any chance of speaking with the patient, and was told that she was undergoing some treatment at the moment and would not be able to talk on the telephone until later in the day. Bond said he would try to phone during his drive through Switzerland, thanked the Herr Doktor and was about to hang up when Kirchtum stopped him.

"There is someone here who would like a word with you, Mr. Bond. Hold on, I'll put her through."

To his surprise, the next voice was that of M's personal assistant, Miss Moneypenny. "James," she said with that hint of affection always present when she spoke to Bond, "how lovely to talk to you."

"Well, Moneypenny. What on earth're you doing at the Mozart?"

"I'm on holiday, like you, and spending a few days in Salzburg. I just thought I'd come up and see May. She's doing very well, James." Moneypenny's voice sounded light and excited.

"Nice of you to think of her. Be careful what you get up to in Salzburg, though, Moneypenny—all those musical people looking at Mozart's house and going to concerts . . ."

"Nowadays they all want to go off to see the locations used in *The Sound of Music*," she laughed.

"Well, take care all the same, Penny. I'm told those tourists are after only one thing from a girl like you."

"Would you were a tourist, then, James," she sighed. Moneypenny still held a special place in her heart for Bond.

After a little more conversation Bond again thanked her for the thoughtful action of visiting May.

His luggage was ready for collection, the windows were open and the sun streamed in. He would take a look around the hotel, check on the car, have some more coffee and get onto the road. As he went down to the foyer he realized how much he needed a holiday. It had been a hard year, and for the first time Bond wondered if he had made the right decision. Perhaps the short trip to his beloved Royale-les-Eaux would have been a better bet, in more ways than one.

He went down to the foyer, pleased to see that the hotel had kept up its excellent standards. It was good to know there were still hotels that provided real service, in a world so often given to the shoddy and easy way out.

He had started for the main doors in order to make his way to the parking area and check the car, when a familiar face slid into the periphery of his vision. He hesitated, turned and gazed absently into the hotel shop window, the better to examine the reflection of a man sitting near the main reception desk.

The man gave no sign of having seen him, as he sat casually glancing through yesterday's *Herald Tribune*. He was short—not even five feet, Bond guessed. Neatly and expensively dressed, he had the look of many small men: one of complete confidence. Bond always mistrusted people of short stature, knowing they had a tendency to overcompensate with pushy ruthlessness, as though it was necessary to prove themselves.

He turned away, having made his identification. The face was known well enough to him—unpleasant features, thin, ferretlike, with the same bright darting eyes as the animal. What, he wondered to himself, was Paul Cordova—or "the Rat" as he was known in underworld circles—doing in Strasbourg? Bond knew him only because, some years ago, there had been a suggestion that the KGB—posing as a United States government agency—had used him to do a particularly nasty piece of work in New York.

Paul "the Rat" Cordova was what the American Mob called an "enforcer" for one of the New York families—a polite way of saying he was a killer, with his photograph and record on the files of the world's major police, security and secret intelligence departments. It was part of Bond's job to know faces like this, even though Cordova moved in criminal rather than intelligence circles. Moreover, Bond did not think of him as "the Rat." To him, the man was "the Poison Dwarf." Another "coincidence"? he wondered.

Going down to the parking area, he checked the Bentley with great care, telling the man on duty that he would be picking it up within half an hour. He refused to let any of the hotel staff move the car, and there had been a certain amount of surliness on his arrival because he would not leave the keys with the concierge. On his way out, Bond could not fail to notice the low, black, wicked-looking Series 3 Porsche 911 Turbo. The rear plates were mud-splattered, though the Swiss Ticino Canton shield showed clearly.

Whoever had shot past him on the motorway, just before the BMW's explosive disintegration, was now at the hotel. Bond's antennae told him that it was time to get out of Strasbourg as quickly as possible. The small cloud of menace had grown a shade larger.

Cordova was not in the foyer when he returned, so, on reaching his room, Bond put through another call to Transworld Exports in London—again using the scrambler. Even on leave it was his duty to report any sightings—particularly of anyone like the Poison Dwarf so far away from his own turf.

Within twenty minutes, Bond was again at the wheel of the Bentley, heading for the German border.

He crossed without incident, skirted Freiburg and by early afternoon again changed countries, going into Switzerland at Basel. A few hours later he was aboard the car train rattling through the St. Gotthard Pass, and by early evening the Bentley had purred through the streets of Locarno and onto the lakeside road, through Ascona, that paradise for artists, both

31

professional and amateur, to the small and pleasing village of Brissago.

In spite of the beauties of the day, the sunlight, clean little Swiss towns and villages, the towering, awesome mountains and breathtaking views, a sense of impending doom remained with Bond as he drove south. At first he put it down to the odd events of the previous day, and the vaguely disconcerting experience of seeing a known New York Mafia hood in Strasbourg. Yet, as the day had progressed, and he neared Lake Maggiore, he wondered if this mood could be due to a slightly dented pride. The girl he had saved, Sukie Tempesta, had appeared so self-assured, calm and unimpressed by Bond's charm that he felt distinctly annoyed. She could, he thought, at least have shown some sort of gratitude. In the event, she had hardly smiled at him.

As the red-brown roofs of the Maggiore lakeside villages came in sight, Bond began to laugh. Suddenly his gloom, and its possible reasons, came into perspective and he saw the pettiness of his attitude. He slid a tape into the stereo system, and, a moment later, the combination of the view and the great Art Tatum rattling out "The Shout" banished the darkness, putting him into a new, happier mood.

Though his favorite part of the country lay around Geneva, Bond also loved this little slice of Switzerland that rubbed shoulders with Italy. As a young man he had lazed around the shores of Lake Maggiore, eaten some of the best meals of his life in Locarno, and once, on a hot moonlit night, with the waters off Brissago alive with lamplit fishing boats, made unforgettable love to an Italian countess in the very ordinary little hotel by the pier.

It was to this hotel—the Mirto Du Lac—that he now headed: a simple, clean and friendly family place, below the church with its arcade of cypresses, and hard by the pier where the lake steamers put in every hour or so.

The padrone greeted him like an old friend, and Bond was soon ensconced in his room, where the little balcony looked out over the lake.

He made himself comfortable, and before unpacking his few needs for the night, dialed the Klinik Mozart. The Herr Direktor was not available so they put him through to one of the junior doctors, who said he was sorry but Mr. Bond could not speak with May. She was resting. There had been a visitor and she was a little tired. For some reason the doctor's words did not ring true. There was a slight hesitation that worried Bond. He asked if May was all right, and the doctor assured him that she was perfectly well, just a little tired.

"This visitor," he went on, "I believe a Miss Moneypenny . . ."

"This is correct." The doctor was the one who sounded most correct.

"I don't suppose you happen to know where she's staying in Salzburg?"

He was sorry but he did not. "I understand she is coming back to see the patient tomorrow," he added.

Bond thanked him and said he would call again. By the time he had showered and changed, it was starting to get dark. Across the lake the sunlight slowly withdrew from Mount Tamaro, and lights went on along the lakeside. Insects began to flock around the glass globes, and one or two couples took seats at the tables outside.

At the moment Bond left his room to go down to the bar that stood in the corner of the restaurant, a black Porsche 911 crept quietly into the forecourt, parking with its nose thrust toward the lake. Its occupant climbed out, carefully locked the car and walked, with neat little steps, back the way he had driven, up toward the church.

It was a good ten minutes later that those sitting outside the Mirto, or, like Bond, in the bar, heard the series of piercing screams.

The steady murmur of talk and laughter petered out as people realized the screams were not some silly girl playing catch and kiss games with her boyfriend. These were shrieks of terror. Several people started toward the door, already some of the men outside were on their feet, others looking around to see where the noise was coming from.

Bond was among those who dashed and pushed

to get outside. The first thing he saw, through the confusion of people, was the Porsche, then the woman, face white, her mouth an open gash that seemed to have taken the place of features, hair flying as she ran down the steps from the churchyard, screaming, hands wild, going to her face, then wringing the air, then clutching her head. Between the screaming she kept shouting, *"Assassinio! Assassinio!"* Murder! Murder! As she yelled the word, one hand would point back, up to the churchyard with its cypresses and rough stones.

Six men beat Bond up the steps, and there were already several others clustered around a small bundle lying across the cobbled path, their voices raised for a moment, then stilled as they came to the object.

Bond moved quietly to the perimeter of this knot of men. Paul "the Rat" Cordova—his Poison Dwarf—lay on his back, knees drawn up, one arm flung outward, his head at an angle, for it seemed to have been almost severed by the single deep slash across the throat.

Bond moved away, pushing through the gathering crowd and heading back down to the lakeside and the hotel. He had never been a man who believed in coincidences. The drowned passengers; the affair at the filling station; the explosion on the motorway; the fact of Cordova's presence—first near him in France, now here on the Swiss-Italian border—were linked. He was the common denominator, and already he

knew that his holiday was shattered. He would telephone London, report and await orders.

But, on reaching the hotel, another surprise
awaited him. There, standing by the reception desk,
looking just as trim as ever, but now wearing a short
blue-tinged leather number, probably a Mer-
enlender, stood yesterday's damsel in distress, Sukie
Tempesta.

— 3 —

Sukie

"JAMES BOND!" The delight appeared to be genuine enough, but, with beautiful women, Bond considered you could never be sure.

"In the flesh." He moved closer, and for the first time really saw her eyes—large, brown with violet flecks, oval, like her face, and set off by exceptionally long, curled and certainly natural lashes. They were eyes, he thought, that could be the undoing of a man, or, coversely, the making of him. His own eyes flicked down to the full firm curve of her breasts under the well-fitting leather.

She stuck out her lower lip, to blow hair from her forehead, as she had done the day before. "I didn't expect to see you again." Her wide mouth tilted in a warm smile. "I'm so glad. I didn't get a chance to thank you, properly. For yesterday, I mean." She bobbed a mock curtsy. "Mr. James Bond, I might well owe you my life. Thank you *very* much. I mean it—*very* much."

He had moved to one side of the reception desk in order to watch her and keep an eye on the main doors. Instinctively, he felt danger close at hand. Danger in being close to Sukie Tempesta, perhaps.

Outside, police moved among the crowd, and the sound of sirens floated down from the main street and church above them. Bond knew he needed his back against a wall at all times now.

She asked him what was going on, and he told her. She shrugged, "It's more commonplace where I spend most of my time. In Rome, murder is a fact of life nowadays, but, somehow, you don't expect it here, in Switzerland."

"It's commonplace anywhere." He tried his most charming smile. "But what are *you* doing here, Miss Tempesta—or is it Mrs., or even Signora?"

She wrinkled her nose, prettily, and raised her eyebrows. "Principessa, actually—if we have to be formal."

Bond lifted an eyebrow. "Principessa Tempesta." He dropped his head in a formal bow.

"Sukie." The wide smile again, and the large eyes, innocent, yet with a minute tinge of mockery. "You call me Sukie, Mr. Bond. Please."

"James."

"James." And at that moment the padrone came

bustling up to complete the paperwork of booking her in. As soon as he saw the title on the registration form everything changed to a hand-wringing, bowing comedy at which Bond could only smile wryly.

"You haven't yet told me what you're doing here," he continued, over the padrone's effusive deference.

"Could I do that over dinner? At least I owe you that." Her hand touched his forearm and he felt the natural exchange of static. Bells of warning rang in his head. No chances, he thought, you must take chances with nobody, particularly with those to whom you are naturally attracted. "Dinner would be fine," he replied, then, once more, asked what she was doing here on Lake Maggiore.

"My little motor car has broken down. There's something very wrong, according to the garage here—which probably means all they'll do is change the plugs. But they say it's going to take days."

"And you're heading for. . . ?"

"Rome, naturally." She blew at her hair again.

"What a happy coincidence," Bond gave another bow, "if I can be of service."

She hesitated a fraction, "Oh, I'm sure you can. Shall we say dinner, down here, in half an hour?"

"I'll be waiting, Principessa."

He thought he saw her nose wrinkle and her tongue poke out, like a naughty schoolgirl's, as she turned to follow the padrone to her room.

In the privacy of his own quarters, Bond telephoned London yet again, giving them the news concerning Cordova. He had the scrambler on, and, as an afterthought, asked them to run a check with the Interpol computer, as well as their own, on the Principessa Sukie Tempesta.

Hoods like Cordova were not nickel and dime men, but contract killers who came at Cartier prices. Principessa Tempesta looked as though she came at a usurious rate of interest. He finally asked the duty officer if they had yet gotten information on the BMW's owner, Herr Tempel of Freiburg. Nothing yet, he was told, but some material had gone to M that afternoon. "You'll hear soon enough if it's important. Have a nice holiday."

Very droll, thought Bond, packing away the scrambling device—a CC500, which could be used on any telephone in the world and allowed only the legitimate receiving party to hear the caller *en clair*. Eavesdroppers of any kind—from the exchange to the professional wiretapper—heard only sounds that were completely indecipherable, even if they tapped in with a compatible system, for each CC500 had to be individually programed. It was standard Service practice nowadays for all officers—on duty or leave—out of the country to carry a CC500, and the access codes were altered daily.

There were ten minutes to spare before he had to meet Sukie—if she was on time—so he washed quickly, rubbing cologne hard into face and hair, then put on a blue cotton jacket over his shirt and went rapidly downstairs and out to the car. There was still a great deal of police activity in the churchyard above, and he could see that a scene-of-crime team had set up lights where Cordova's body had been discovered.

Inside the car he waited for the courtesy lights to click off before activating the switch on the main lighting panel, allowing the concealed compartment to drop down below the facia.

Slipping off his jacket, he buckled the compact holster in place, checking the 9mm ASP before getting the jacket on again and securing the baton's holster to his belt. He had no idea what was going on around him, but it had already cost at least two lives— probably more. Care would ensure that he did not end up as the next cadaver, for he was now more than certain that the proximity of these deaths was no accident. Coolly, Bond had already accepted that some unseen menace was stalking him—and him alone.

To his immense surprise, Sukie was already at the bar when he got back into the hotel. "Like a dutiful woman I didn't order anything while I waited." She blew at her hair again—it was like a nervous tic.

"I prefer dutiful women." Bond slid onto the bar stool next to her, turning it slightly so that he had a clear view of anyone coming through the big glass doors at the front. "What'll you drink?"

"Oh, no, tonight's on me. In honor of your saving

my honor, James." Again the hand lightly brushed his arm, and he felt the same electricity.

Bond capitulated, "Well, we're in Ticino where they think grappa is good liquor, so I'd best stick to the comic drinks—a Campari soda, if I may."

She ordered the same, then the padrone bustled over with the menu. It was very *famiglia*, very *semplice*, he explained. It would make a change, Bond said, and Sukie asked him to order for them both. He said he would be difficult and change the menu around a little, starting with the *Melone al kirsch*, asking them to serve his plain, without the kirsch—Bond disliked any food soused in alcohol, and deplored the current fashion in many English restaurants for cooking practically everything in wine, or worse, vermouth. He was pleased to note that Sukie agreed, pulling a face to indicate the fact.

"For the entrée there's really only one dish, pasta excepted, in these parts, you'll agree. . . ?"

"The *coscia d' agnello?*" She smiled as he nodded. In the north these spiced lamb chops were known as Lamm-Gigot. Here, among the Ticinese, they were less delicate to the palate but made delicious by the use of much garlic. Like Bond, Sukie refused any vegetables but accepted the plain green salad that he also ordered, together with a bottle of Frecciarossa Bianco, apparently the best white wine they could supply. Bond had taken one look at the champagnes and pronounced them undrinkable, but "probably reasonable for making a dressing," at which Sukie laughed. Her laugh was, Bond thought, the least attractive thing about her, a shade harsh, difficult to detect as genuine.

When they were seated, Bond wasted no time in making an offer to help her on her journey. "I'm leaving for Rome in the morning. If you want a lift, I'd be very pleased. That is if the Principe won't be offended at a commoner bringing you home."

She gave a little pout, "He's in no position to be offended. Principe Pasquale Tempesta died last year."

"I'm sorry, I . . ."

She gave a dismissive wave of the right hand, "Oh, don't be sorry. He was eighty-three. We were married for two years; it was convenient, that's all." She did not smile or try to make light of it.

"A marriage of convenience?"

"No, it was just convenient. I like good things. He had money; he was old; he needed someone to keep him warm at night—he could do precious little else. In the Bible didn't King David take a young girl—Abishag—to keep him warm?"

"I believe so. My upbringing was a touch Calvinistic, yet I seem to recall the Lower Fourth sniggering over that story."

"Well, that's what I was, Pasquale Tempesta's Abishag, and he enjoyed it. Now, I enjoy what he left me."

"For an Italian you speak excellent English."

"I should." The smile again, and then the laugh, a shade more mellow this time. "I *am* English."

"You speak excellent Italian, then."

"And French, and German." She reached forward, putting out a hand to cover his as it lay on the table beside his glass. "Don't worry, James, I'm not a witch. But I can spot nosy questions, like all those you put to me yesterday, however subtly. Comes from the nuns, then living with Pasquale's people."

"Nuns?"

"I'm a good convent-educated girl, James. You know about girls who've been educated in convents?"

"A fair amount."

She gave another little pout. "I was pretty well brainwashed. Daddy was a broker, all very ordinary: home counties; mock-Tudor house; two cars; one scandal. Daddy got caught out with some funny checks and drew five years in an open prison. Collapse of stout family. I'd just finished at the convent, and was all set to go to Oxford. That was out, so I answered an ad in *The Times*—nanny, with a mound of privileges, to an Italian family of good birth: Pasquale's son, as it happened. It's an old title, like all the surviving Italian nobility, but with one difference— they still have property and money."

To cut the amusing story short, for she took a long time in its telling, the Tempesta family had taken their new English nanny into the family as one of their own. The old man, the Principe, had become a second father to her. She became very fond of him, so, when he proposed a marriage—which he described as *comodo* as opposed to *comodita*—Sukie, whose maiden name was Susan Destry, saw a certain wisdom in taking up the offer.

Yet even in that she showed shrewdness, careful to be certain that the marriage would in no way deprive Pasquale's two sons of their rightful inheritance. "It did, to some extent, but they're both wealthy, and successful in their own right, and they put forward no objections. You know old Italian families, James. Papa's happiness; Papa's rights; respect for Papa . . ."

Bond asked in what way the two sons had become successful, and she hesitated a fraction too long before airily saying, "Oh, business. They own companies and that kind of thing, and, yes, James, I'll take you up on your offer of a ride to Rome. Thank you."

They were halfway through the lamb when the padrone came hurrying forward, excused himself to Sukie, and bent to whisper that there was an urgent telephone call for Bond, pointing toward the bar, which had its phone off the hook.

"Bond," he said quietly into the receiver.

"James, you somewhere private?" He recognized the voice immediately—Bill Tanner, M's Chief of Staff.

"No. I'm having dinner."

"This is urgent. Very urgent. Could you. . . ?"

"Of course." He closed the line and went back to the table to make his apologies to Sukie. "It won't take long." He told her about May being ill in the Klinik. "They want me to ring them back."

In his room he set up the CC500 and called London. Bill Tanner came on the line straight away. "Don't say anything, James, just listen. The instructions are from M, do you accept that?"

"Of course." He had no alternative, if Bill Tanner said he was speaking for the Chief of the Secret Service. Bond's discipline was obedience, like a monk to his abbot.

"You're to stay where you are and take great care." There was anxiety in Tanner's voice.

"I'm due in Rome tomorrow, I . . . ."

"Listen to me, James. Rome's coming to you. You, I repeat *you*, are in gravest hazard. Genuine danger. We can't get anyone to you quickly, to watch your back, so you'll have to do it for yourself. You stay put and stay tight. Understand?"

"I understand." When Bill Tanner spoke of Rome coming to him, he meant Steve Quinn, the Service resident in Rome. The same Steve Quinn with whom he had planned to spend a couple of days. He asked why Rome was coming to him.

"To put you fully in the picture. Brief you. Try to get you out." He heard Tanner take a quick breath at the other end of the line. "I can't stress the danger

46

strongly enough, old friend. The Chief suspected problems before you left, but we only got the hard intelligence in the last hour." M had flown to Geneva. Rome—Steve Quinn—was on his way there to be briefed, then he would come straight to Bond. "Be with you before lunch. In the meantime, trust nobody. For God's sake just stay close."

"I'm with the Tempesta girl now. Promised her a ride to Rome. What's the form on her?" Bond crisp and terse.

"We haven't got it all, but the people to whom she's related seem clean enough. Certainly not connected with the Honored Society. Treat her with care, though. Don't let her get behind you."

"I was thinking of the opposite, as a matter of fact," Bond's mouth moved into a hard smile.

Tanner ordered him to keep her at the hotel. "Stall her about Rome, but don't alert her. You really don't know who are your friends and who your enemies. Rome'll give you the full strength tomorrow. Lock your door; keep your back to the wall."

"We won't be able to leave until late morning, I'm afraid," he told Sukie, once back at the table. "That was a business chum who's been to see my old housekeeper. He's passing through here tomorrow morning, and I really can't miss the chance of seeing him."

She said it did not matter. "I was hoping for a lie-in tomorrow anyway." Could he detect an invitation in her voice?

They talked on, had coffee and a *fine* in the dining room, neat with its red and white checkered table-cloths, gleaming cutlery, and the two serious wait-resses, who went about their business as though serving writs instead of food. The girls, he thought, probably came from the north. There, the stolidness of the waitress often belied a fire of good clean lust lurking beneath the sensible shoes and uniforms. At least Bond had often discovered so in his youth.

Sukie suggested they should go outside, to sit at one of the tables fronting the Mirto, but Bond made an excuse not to. "Mosquitoes and midges tend to congregate around the lights," he said. "You'll end up with that lovely skin blotched. Safer indoors."

She asked what kind of business he was in, and he answered n his usual vague way, which she appeared nonetheless to accept. They talked of towns and cities they both enjoyed, and of food and drink.

"Perhaps I can take you to dinner in Rome," Bond suggested. "Without seeming ungrateful, I think we can get something a shade more interesting at Papa Giovanni's or Augustea."

"I'd love it. It's a change to talk to someone who knows Europe well. Pasquale's family are very Ro-man, I fear. They don't really see much further than the Appian Way."

In all, it was a pleasant evening, though Bond had to put up a show of being relaxed after hearing the

48

news from London. Now he had to get through the night.

They went up together, with Bond offering to escort Sukie to her room. They reached the door, and he had no doubt as to what would happen. She came into his arms easily enough, but, when he kissed her, she did not respond, her lips closed and tight, her body rigid.

So, he thought, one of those. But he tried again, if only because he wanted to keep her in sight. This time she pulled away, gently putting her fingers to his mouth, "I'm sorry, James. But no." There was the ghost of a smile as she said, "I'm a good convent girl, remember. But that's not the only reason. If you're serious, be patient. Now, goodnight, and thank you for the lovely evening."

"I should thank *you*, Principessa," he said with a shade of formality, watched as she closed her door, then went slowly to his own room, swallowed a couple of Benzedrine tablets and prepared to sit up all night, ready for anything.

— 4 —

The Head Hunt

Steve Quinn was a big man, tall, broad, bearded and with an expansive personality—"a big, bearded bastard," Steve's wife, the petite, blonde Tabitha, was often heard to remark. Not the usual kind of person who made it to a responsible position in the Service. The Service preferred what it liked to call "invisible men"—ordinary, gray people who could vanish into a crowd like illusionists.

Now, Bond—wearing only the silk Happi-coat— watched from the shadows of his half-closed shutters as the big, bearded bastard alighted from a hired car and walked toward the hotel entrance.

A few seconds later, the telephone rang and Bond said they should allow Mr. Quarterman up to his room. Quarterman was the name under which Quinn traveled.

The man from Rome was inside, with the door

closed and locked, almost before the knock had died in the air.

Quinn did not speak immediately, going straight to the window, glancing down onto the stretch of forecourt and the lake steamer that had just docked to disgorge its local and tourist passengers. The sight of the sheer magnificent beauty usually took people's breath away when they disembarked, but this morning the loud yah-yah-yahing of an affected English-woman's voice could be heard even in Bond's room—"I wonder what there is to see here, darling?"

Bond scowled, and Quinn gave a little twisted smile almost hidden by his beard. He looked at the detritus of breakfast still on its tray and mouthed a few words, asking if the place was clean.

"Spent the night going over it. Nothing in the telephone, or anywhere else."

Quinn nodded, "Okay."

Bond asked why they could not have flown Geneva up to him—they usually spoke of Service residents by the name of their area of influence.

"Because Geneva's got problems of his own," Steve Quinn's finger stabbed out toward Bond, "but not a patch on *your* personal problems, James."

"Talk then. The Chief met you for a briefing?"

"Right. I've done what I can, within limits. Geneva doesn't like it, but two of my people should be here by now to watch your back. M wants you in London—in one piece if possible."

"So, there *is* someone on my tail." He sounded

unconcerned, but pictures of the shattered car on the motorway and the American hood's body lying in the churchyard reeled through his mind.

Quinn lowered his considerable bulk into a chair. When he spoke it was low, almost a whisper. "No," he said, "you haven't got someone on your tail. It seems to us that you've got just about every willing terrorist organization, criminal gang and unfriendly foreign intelligence service right up your ass. There is, to use a gangland expression, a contract out for you. A unique contract. Somebody has made every alien organization—to coin a phrase—an offer they can't refuse."

Bond gave a hard half smile. "Okay, break it to me gently. What am I worth?"

"Oh, they don't want all of you. Just your head."

Quinn began. It appeared that M had received some indication about two weeks before Bond went on leave. "The firm that controls South London tried to spring Bernie Brazier from the Island." In plain language, this meant that the most powerful underworld organization in South London had tried to get one Bernie Brazier out of the high-security prison at Parkhurst, on the Isle of Wight. Brazier was doing life for the cold-blooded killing of a quite notorious London underworld figure, noted for his professional skills. Scotland Yard knew he had carried out at least twelve murders for money, but could not prove it. In short, Bernie Brazier was Britain's top "mechanic," which is a very polite name for hired killer.

"The escape was bungled. A real dog's breakfast. Then, after it was all over, friend Brazier wanted to do a deal," Quinn continued, "and, as you know, the Met don't take kindly to deals. So he asked to see somebody from the sisters"—he spoke of their sister Service, MI5. This had been refused, but the details were passed to M, who sent the Grand Inquisitor to Parkhurst Prison, where Brazier claimed that he was being sprung for a particular job, that it was important to the country's security and that he had details. But, in return for the goods, he required a new identity, in the sun, with money to singe if not actually to burn.

Bond remained oddly detached, for the scenario, as Quinn explained it, had a dreamlike, nightmarish quality. He knew the devil incarnate in M would promise the world for hard intelligence, and then give the source of supply a very small plot of earth. So it had been. Another pair of interrogators had gone to Parkhurst and had a long talk with Brazier. Then M had taken the trip, himself, to make the promises.

"And Bernie told all?" he finally asked.

"Some of it. The rest was to come once he was nicely tucked away in some tropical paradise with enough birds and booze to give him a coronary within a year." Quinn's face went very hard. "The day after M's visit they found Bernie in his cell—hanged with piano wire."

From outside came the sound of children at play near the jetty, the toot of one of the lake boats and, far away, the drone of a light airplane. Bond asked what they had gotten from the late Bernie Brazier.

"That you were the target for this unique contract. A kind of competition."

"Competition?"

"There are rules, it appears, and the winner is the group that physically brings your head to the organizers—on a silver charger, no less. Any bona fide criminal, terrorist or intelligence agency can enter. They have to be accepted by the organizers. The starting date was four days ago, and there's a time limit. Three months. Winner gets ten million Swiss."

Bond gave a low whistle.

"Quite." Quinn did not smile.

"Who in heaven's name. . . ?" Bond started.

"M discovered the answer to that less than twenty-four hours ago, with the help of the Metropolitan Police. About a week back, they pulled in half of the South London mob, and let M's heavy squad have a go. It paid off—or M's paying off, I don't quite know which. I do know that four major London gangland chiefs are pleading for round-the-clock protection, and I guess they need it. The fifth one"—he mentioned the name—"laughed at M and walked out of the slammer. I gather they found him last night. He was not in a good state."

When Quinn went into the details of this particular man's demise, even Bond felt queasy. "Jesus . . ."

"Saves," Quinn showed not a shred of humor. "One can but hope He's saved that poor bastard. Forensic say he took an unconscionable time a'dying."

"And who's organized this grisly competition?"

"It's even got a name, by the way," Steve Quinn interrupted in a somewhat offhand manner. "It's called the Head Hunt. No consolation prizes, just the big one. M reckons that around thirty professional killers went through the starting gate . . ."

"Who's behind it?"

Quinn nodded, making placating movements with his hands. "In general, your old friends the Special Executive for Counterintelligence, Terrorism, Revenge and Extortion—SPECTRE. In particular, the inheritor of the Blofeld dynasty, their leader, with whom you've had one nasty brush, M tells me . . ."

"Tamil Rahani. The so-called Colonel Tamil Rahani."

"Who will be the late Tamil Rahani in a matter of three to four months. Hence the time limit."

Bond was silent for a minute. He was fully aware of how dangerous Tamil Rahani could be. They had never really discovered how he had managed to take over as chief executive of SPECTRE, that organization which seemed to have always kept its leadership embedded in a sort of right of succession within the Blofeld family. But certainly the inventive, ruthless, brilliant strategist of terror, Tamil Rahani, *had* become SPECTRE's leader. He could see the man now—dark-skinned, muscular, radiating self-discipline and a controlled dynamism. Short, full of fire and guile. A smooth, ruthless and internationally powerful leader.

He recalled the last time he had seen him, drifting by parachute over Geneva—Tamil Rahani's great forte as a terrorist commander was that he led from the front. He had tried to have Bond killed a month or so after that last meeting. Since then there had been few sightings, but 007 could well believe in this bizarre competition SPECTRE titled the Head Hunt—especially if it was the brain-child of the truly sinister Tamil Rahani.

"You're implying the man's on his way out? Dying?"

"There was a sudden and dangerous escape by parachute . . ." Quinn did not look him in the eyes.

"Yes."

"Information is that he jarred his spine on landing. In turn this caused problems. The man has a cancer affecting the spinal cord. Apparently M knows of six specialists who've seen him. There is no hope. Within four months, Tamil Rahani's going to be the late Tamil Rahani."

Bond nodded. "Who's involved? Apart from SPECTRE, who am I up against?"

Quinn slid a hand down his dark beard. "M's working on it. A lot of your old enemies, of course,

56

whatever they call the former Department V of the KGB these days—what used to be SMERSH . . ."

"Department Eight of Directorate S: KGB," Bond snapped.

Quinn went on as though he had not heard, ". . . Also practically every known terrorist organization, from the old Red Brigade to the Puerto Rican FALN—the Armed Forces for National Liberation. With ten million Swiss francs as the star prize you've attracted a lot of attention."

"You mentioned the underworld."

"Of course—British, French, German, at least three Mafia families and, I fear, the Union Corse. Since the demise of your ally, Marc-Ange Draco, they've been less than helpful . . ."

"All right!" Bond stopped him, sharply.

Steve Quinn lifted his large body from the chair. There was no effort, as is so often the case with heavy men, just a fast movement, a second between being seated and facing Bond, one large hand reaching out and holding 007's shoulder. "Yes. Yes, I know. This is going to be a bitch." He hesitated, as though something even more unpleasant had to be said. "There's one other thing you've got to know about Head Hunt . . ."

Bond shook off the hand. Quinn had been tactless in reminding him of the special relationship he had once nurtured between the Service and the Union

Corse—that Cosa Nostra–like underworld link which could be even more deadly than the Mafia. Bond's contacts with the Union Corse had led to his marriage, followed quickly by the death of his bride, Marc-Ange Draco's daughter. "What other thing? You've made it plain I cannot trust anybody—can I even trust you?" With a sense of disgust, Bond realized he meant the last remark. Nobody. He could not even trust Steve Quinn—the Service's man in Rome.

"It's to do with SPECTRE's rules for Head Hunt." Quinn's face would have done credit to Mount Rushmore. "The organizations, or criminal fraternities, who've applied to enter the competition are restricted to putting one man in the field—one only. The latest information is that four of these contestants have already died violently within the past twenty-four hours—one of them only a few hundred meters from where we're sitting."

"Tempel, Cordova, and a couple of thugs on the Ostend Ferry."

"Right. The ferry passengers were two opposing London gang representatives—South London and the West End. Tempel had known links with the Red Army faction—he was an underworld-trained hood, with money and influence, a barroom politician who thought there were rich pickings in the politics of terrorism. The American, Paul Cordova, you know about."

All four of them, Bond thought, had already been

near to him, and very close indeed when they were murdered. What were the odds on that being a coincidence? Aloud, he asked Quinn what M's orders were.

"You're to get back to London at the speed of light. We honestly haven't the manpower available to look after you loose on the Continent. My own two boys'll see you to the nearest airport and then take care of the car . . ."

"No." Bond whirled on him. "No, I'll get the car back, nobody else is going to take care of it for me—right?"

Quinn shrugged. "Your funeral. You're terribly vulnerable in that vehicle."

But Bond did not appear to notice. He was already moving about the room, neatly finishing his packing, yet all the time his senses were centered on Quinn. Trust nobody: Right, he would not even trust this man. "Your boys?" he asked. "Give me a rundown."

Quinn nodded in the direction of the window. "They're out there. Look for yourself," he said, going toward the shuttered balcony, peering through the louvered slats.

Bond placed himself just behind the big man. "There," Quinn said. "One standing by the rocks, in the blue shirt. The other's in the silver Renault, parked at the end of the row of cars." It was a Renault 25 V6i. Not Bond's favorite kind of car. If he played his cards properly he could outrun that pair with ease. "I wanted information on one other person." He stepped back into the center of the room. "An English girl who's inherited an Italian title . . ."

"Tempesta?" There was a sneer on Quinn's lips. Bond nodded.

"M doesn't think she's part of the game, though she could be bait. He says you should take care—what he actually said was, 'exercise caution.' She's around, I gather."

"Very much so. I've promised to give her a lift to Rome."

"Dump her!" An order.

"We'll see. Okay, Quinn, if that's all you have for me, I'll sort out my route home. It could be scenic."

Quinn nodded and stuck out his hand, which Bond ignored. "Good luck. You're going to need it."

"I don't altogether believe in luck. Really I believe in only one thing—myself."

Quinn frowned, nodded and left Bond to make his final preparations. Speed was essential, but his main thought at this moment was what he should do about Sukie Tempesta. She was there, an unknown quantity, yet he felt she could be used somehow. A hostage, perhaps? The Principessa Tempesta would make an adequate hostage, a shield even, if he felt that ruthless.

As though by some act of clairvoyance, the telephone rang and Sukie's voice came, mellow, on the line, "I was wondering what time you wanted to leave, James?"

"Whenever it suits you. I'm almost ready."

She laughed, and the harshness seemed to have gone—there was some humor in her voice as she said she only had to finish packing, "Fifteen minutes at the most. You want to eat here, before we leave?"

Bond said he'd prefer to stop for a snack en route if she did not mind, then added, "Look, Sukie, I've got a very small problem. A minor thing, but it might effect our journey—the odd detour. May I come and talk to you before we go?"

"To my room?"

"It would be better."

"It could also cause a small scandal for a well-brought-up convent girl."

"I can promise you there'll be no scandal. Shall we say ten minutes' time?"

"If you insist." She was not being unpleasant, just a shade more formal than before.

"It's quite important, and you truly need not concern yourself with any scandal. I'll be with you in ten minutes."

Hardly had he put down the telephone and snapped the locks on his case when the instrument rang again.

"Mr. Bond?" He recognized the booming voice of Herr Doktor Kirchtum, director of the Klinik Mozart, but the voice appeared to have lost its ebullience.

"Herr Direktor?" Bond heard the note of anxiety in his own tone.

"I'm sorry, Mr. Bond. It is not good news . . ."

"May!"

"Your patient, Mr. Bond. She is vanished. The police are here with me now. I'm sorry not to have made contact sooner. But she is vanished—with the friend who visited yesterday, the Moneypenny lady. There has been a telephone call and the police wish to speak with you. She has been, how do you say it? Napped . . ."

"Kidnapped? May, kidnapped, and Moneypenny?" A thousand thoughts went through his head, but only one of them made sense. Someone had done his homework very well. Kidnapping May could just possibly be a byproduct of the kidnapping of Moneypenny, whose situation always made her a likely target. What was more likely, though, was that one of the Head Hunt entrants wanted Bond under close control, and how better than to lead him in a search for May and Moneypenny?

— 5 —

Nannie

ALL THINGS BEING CONSIDERED—Bond thought—Sukie Tempesta showed that she was an uncommonly cool lady.

He had showered and shaved before Quinn's arrival, so now he worked out a plan to deal with Sukie as he dressed—casual slacks, with his favorite soft leather moccasins and a sea island cotton shirt, over which he threw a battledress-style gray Oscar Jacobson Alcantara jacket. The jacket was mainly to hide the 9mm ASP. He then placed his case, and the two briefcases, near the door, checked the ASP and went quickly downstairs where he settled both his own and Sukie's accounts with a credit card, returning with equal speed to the second floor, going straight to her room.

Of course she had Gucci luggage—one medium-

63

size case, a dressing case and the briefcase. They stood in a neat line near the door, which she opened to his knock. She was back in the Calvin Klein jeans, this time with a black silk shirt that looked very Christian Dior.

He gently pushed her back into the room, though she did open her mouth to protest, saying she was ready to leave, but his face was set in a serious mask that made her ask, "James, what is it? Something's really wrong, isn't it?"

"I'm sorry, Sukie. Yes. Very serious for me, and it could be dangerous for you also."

"I don't understand . . ."

"I have to do certain things you might not like. You see, I've been threatened . . ."

"Threatened? How threatened?" She continued to back away.

"I can't go into details now, but it's clear to me—and others—that there's a possibility you could be involved."

"Me? Involved with what, James? Threatening you?"

"It *is* a serious business, Sukie. Don't be fooled, my life's at risk, and we met in rather dubious circumstances . . ."

"Oh, dubious my eye. What was dubious about it? Except for those unpleasant young muggers?"

"It appeared that I came along at a fortunate moment. It seems I saved you from something unpleas-

64

ant. Then your car breaks down—conveniently near where I'm staying. Being, I trust, a gentleman, I offer you a lift to Rome. Some people might see this as a scenario for a setup, with me as the target."

"But I don't—"

"I'm sorry, I—"

"You can't take me to Rome?" Her voice was level. "I understand, James. Don't worry about it, I'll find some way, but it does present me with a little problem of my own . . ."

"Oh, you're coming with me—maybe even to Rome eventually. I have no alternative. I *have* to take you—even if it's as a hostage. I must have a little insurance with me. You'll be my policy."

He paused, letting it sink in, then, to his surprise, she smiled. "Well, I've never been a hostage before. It'll be a new experience." She looked down and saw the gun in his hand. "Oh, James! Melodrama? You don't need that. I'm on a kind of holiday anyway. I really don't mind being your hostage, if it's necessary." She paused, her face registering a fascinated pleasure. "It could even be exciting, and I'm all for excitement."

"The kind of people I'm up against are about as exciting as tarantulas, and lethal as sidewinders. I hope what's going to happen now isn't going to be too nasty for you, Sukie. I have no other option, and I *have* to be very careful. I promise you this is no game. You're to do everything I say, and do it very slowly.

65

No disrespect is intended, but just turn around—
right around, like a model—with your hands on your
head."

Initially, he was looking for two things, the
makeshift weapon or the one more cunningly concealed. She wore a small cameo brooch, holding together the neck of her shirt. He made her unpin the
brooch and throw it gently onto the bed, where her
shoulder bag lay. The brooch was followed by her
shoes.

He kept the cameo—it looked safe, but techni-
cians could do nasty things with brooch pins. All his
examining moves were accomplished deftly with one
hand, while the ASP stayed well back in the other.

The shoes were clean—he knew every possible
permutation with shoes—as was her belt. He apologized for the indignity, but her clothes and person
were the first priorities. If she carried nothing suspicious he could deal with the luggage later, making
sure it was kept out of harm's way until they stopped
somewhere, so he emptied the shoulder bag onto the
bed. The usual junk spilled out onto the white quilt—
checkbook, credit cards, cash, Kleenex, comb, a small
bottle of pills, about twenty-five crumpled Amex and
Visa receipts, a small scent spray—Cacharel Anais
Anais—lipstick and a gold compact, plus a dozen or
so other miscellaneous, useless items, thrust into the
bag out of habit or sentiment.

He kept the comb, some book matches, a small

sewing kit from the Plaza Athénée, the scent spray, lipstick and compact. Comb, book matches and sewing kit were immediately adaptable weapons for close-quarter work. The spray, lipstick and compact needed closer inspection. In his time he had known scent sprays to contain liquids more deadly than even the most repellent scent; lipsticks to house razor-sharp curved blades, propellants of one kind or another, even hypodermic syringes; and powder compacts to conceal miniature radios, or worse.

She was more embarrassed than angry about having to strip. Her body was the color of rich creamed coffee, smooth and regular, with the kind of tan you can get only through patience, the right lotions, a correct regimen of sun and nudity. It was the sort of body that men dreamed of finding alive and wriggling in their beds: a designer body.

He would have given much to examine the body in detail, but now was not the time, so Bond went through the jeans and shirt, making doubly sure there was nothing inserted in linings or stitching. When he was satisfied, he apologized again, told her to get dressed and then call down to the concierge. She was to use exact words—that the luggage was ready in her room and in Mr. Bond's. It was to be taken straight to Mr. Bond's car.

Sukie did as she was told, and as she put down the receiver, gave a little shake of the head, "I'll do exactly as I'm told, James. You're obviously desperate, and you're also undoubtedly a professional of some kind. I'm not a fool. I like you. I'll do anything, within reason, but I also have a problem." Her voice shook slightly, as though the whole experience had unnerved her.

Bond nodded, indicating that she should tell him her problem.

"I've an old school friend in Cannobio, just along the lakeshore . . ."

"Yes, I know Cannobio, one-horse Italian holiday resort. Picturesque in a guide-booky kind of way. Not far."

"I took the liberty of telling her we'd pick her up on our way through. I was supposed to do it last night—meet her, that is. She's waiting at that rather lovely church on the lakeside—the Madonna della Pieta. Going to be there from noon onward."

"Can we put her off? Telephone her?"

She shook her head. "After I arrived, with the car problems, I telephoned the hotel where she was supposed to be staying. That was last night. She hadn't arrived. I called her again after dinner, and she was waiting there. They were booked up. She was going in search of somewhere else. You'd said we might be late setting off so I just told her to be at the Madonna della Pieta from twelve noon. I didn't think of getting her to call back . . ."

She was interrupted by the padrone himself, arriving to collect the luggage.

68

Bond thanked him, said they would be down in a few minutes and turned his mind to the problem. There was a lot of road to cover whatever he did, and his aim was to get safely to Salzburg and the Klinik Mozart, where there would be a certain amount of police protection in the current search for May and Moneypenny. He had no desire to go into Italy at all, and, from what he could recall of the center of Cannobio, it was the perfect place for a setup. The lakeside road, with the square in front of the Madonna della Pieta, was always busy: plenty of people, and a lot of traffic—both tourist and local, for Cannobio was a thriving industrial center as well as a lakeside paradise for holidaymakers.

The area in front of the church was ideal territory for one man—or a team on a motorcycle—to make a kill. Was Sukie, knowingly or not, putting him on the spot?

"What's her name? This old school friend?" he asked.

"Norrich." She spelled it out for him. "Nannette Norrich. Everyone calls her 'Nannie,' as in babies, not goats. Norrich Petrochemicals, that's Daddy."

Bond nodded as though he had already guessed. "We'll have to leave her. She'll just have to stew. Sorry."

He took her by the elbow, firmly to let her know that he was in charge.

In the back of his head, Bond already knew that the trip to Cannobio would hold him up for an hour—thirty minutes there, and another half hour back—before he could head off toward the frontier, and Austria.

It would mean two hostages, not one. He could position them in the car to make a hit more difficult, and there was also comfort in the fact that it was *his* head that would gain the prize. Whoever struck would do it on a lonely stretch of road, or, possibly, during a night stop. It was easy enough to sever a human head. You did not even have to be very strong. A flexi-saw—like a bladed metal garrote—would do it in no time. The only thing you did need was a certain amount of privacy. Nobody would have a go in front of the Madonna della Pieta, Cannobio, on the Italian side of Lake Maggiore.

Outside, the padrone stood, at the rear of the British Racing Green Mulsanne Turbo, waiting patiently with the luggage.

Out of the corner of his eye, Bond saw Steve Quinn's man, the tall one standing above the rocks, begin to saunter casually back along the cars toward the Renault. The man did not even look in his direction, but kept his head down, as though searching for dropped coins. He was tall, with the face of a Greek statue that had been exposed to a great deal of time and weather.

Bond contrived to keep Sukie between himself and the car, reaching forward from behind her to unlock the trunk.

70

When the luggage was stowed, they all shook hands with a certain gravity, and he escorted Sukie to the front passenger side. "I want you to fasten the seatbelt, then keep your hands in sight on the facia," he smiled. She smiled back, and along the line of cars the Renault grumbled into life.

Bond settled into the driving seat with engine running. "Sukie, please don't do anything stupid. I promise that I can act much faster than you. Don't make me do anything I might regret."

She smiled very prettily. "I'm the hostage. I know my place. Don't worry."

They backed out, headed up the ramp and, seven minutes later, crossed the Italian frontier with the minimum of fuss.

"If you haven't noticed, there's a car behind us," her voice quavered slightly.

"That's right." Bond gave a grim little smile. "They're babysitting us, but I don't want that kind of protection. We'll throw them off eventually."

He had told her that Nannie would have to be handled with care—not given any details, except the option that she could go on to Rome under her own steam. Plans had changed and they had to get to Salzburg in a hurry. "Leave it to her. Let her make up her own mind. Be apologetic, but try to put her off," he cautioned. "Follow me?"

She nodded.

There was a lot of action around the Madonna

della Pieta when they arrived—tourists and traffic, as
he had expected—but there, standing by a small suitcase, looking supremely elegant, was a very tall girl
with hair the color of a moonless night pulled back
into a severe bun. She wore a patterned cotton dress,
which the breeze caught for a second, blowing it
against her body to reveal the outline of long, slim
thighs, rounded belly and well-proportioned hips. In
spite of the hair, and an attempt to make her appear a
Plain Jane, the body—what one could see of it—revealed possible depths that any red-blooded male
would be eager to plumb.

"My, how super! A Bentley. I adore Bentleys."
She grinned when Sukie called her over to the passenger side of the car.

"Nannie, meet James. We have a problem." She
explained the situation, just as Bond had instructed
her. All the time, he watched Nannie's face—calm,
rather thin features, granny glasses, behind which a
pair of dark gray eyes peered out brightly, full of
intelligence. The long dark hair looked as though it
had been cut by someone who should have known
better, and her eyebrows were unfashionably
plucked, giving the attractive features a look of almost permanent sweet expectation.

"Well, I'm easy." Nannie had a low-pitched drawl,
not unpleasant, certainly not affected, but giving the
impression that she did not believe a word of Sukie's

72

tale. "It *is* a holiday after all—Rome or Salzburg—it mattereth not. Anyway, I adore Mozart."

"Are you coming with us, Nannie?" Bond felt vulnerable, out in the open, and could not allow the girls to start chattering—that could go on for hours. His voice pushed urgency into the situation.

"Of course. Wouldn't miss it for the world." Nannie had the door open, but Bond stopped her. "Luggage in the boot," he said a little sharply, then very quietly to Sukie, "hands in sight, like before. This is too important for games."

She gave a nod of understanding, placing her hands above the facia, as Bond got out and watched Nannie Norrich put her case into the trunk. "Shoulder bag as well, please." He smiled his most charming smile.

"I shall need it. On the road, I'll need it. Why. . . ?"

"Please, Nannie, be a good girl. The problems Sukie told you about are mine, and they're dangerous. I can't have *any* luggage in the car. When the time comes, I'll check your bag and let you have it back, okay?"

She gave a funny little worried turn of the head and a puzzled look, but did as she was told. The Renault, Bond noticed, was parked ahead of them, the engine idling. Good, they thought he planned to route through Italy.

"Nannie, we've only just met and I don't want you to get any ideas, but I have to be slightly indelicate," he said quietly. The trunk was still open, he could see Sukie plainly through the rear window and there were a lot of people around, but what he had to do was necessary. "Don't struggle or yell at me. I have to touch you, but be assured I'm not taking liberties. Lives are in danger."

With fast expert movements he ran his hands over her body, using fingertips and trying not to make it embarrassing for the girl. "I don't know you," he said as he went through the quick frisk, "but my life's at risk, so if you get into the car you're also in danger. As a stranger you could also be dangerous to me. Understand?"

To his surprise, she smiled at him. "Actually, I found that rather pleasant. I *don't* understand, but I still liked it. We should do it again sometime. In private."

They settled back in the car and he asked Nannie to fasten her seatbelt in the rear, telling them there was fast driving ahead.

He started the engine again and waited, both for the road traffic to clear and to be certain there was space free of pedestrians, and vehicles, behind him. When things seemed right, he slid the Bentley into reverse, spun the wheel, banged at accelerator and brake, slewing the car backward into a skid, bringing the rear around in a half circle, then roaring off, cutting between a peeping VW and a truckload of vegetables—much to the wrath of the drivers.

Through the mirror he could see the Renault in trouble and taken by surprise. He increased speed as soon as they were through the restricted zone, and began to take the bends and winds of the lakeside road at expert, if dangerous, speed.

At the frontier he told the guards that he thought they were being followed by brigands, making much of his spare passport—the diplomatic one always carried against emergencies.

The carabinieri were suitably impressed, called him *Eccellenza,* bowed to the ladies and promised to question the occupants of the Renault with vigor.

"Do you always drive like that?" Nannie hummed from the rear, "I suppose you do. You strike me as a fast-cars, horses and women kind of fellow. Action man."

Bond did not comment. Violent man, he thought, concentrating on the driving, allowing the girls to slip into talk of schooldays, parties and men.

There were some problems—particularly when the girls wished to use restrooms—but they managed it twice during the afternoon, by stopping at service areas with Bond positioning the car so that he had full view of any pay telephones, and of the restroom doors. He let them go one at a time, making pleasantly veiled threats as to what would happen to the one left in the car, should either of them do anything

75

foolish. His own bladder had to be kept under control, but just before they started on the long, awesome mountain route that would take them into Austria, they rested together at a roadside café and had food. It was here that Bond took the chance of leaving the girls alone.

When he returned they both looked as though butter would not melt, though they seemed surprised when he popped a couple of Benzedrine tablets with his coffee.

"We were wondering . . ." Nannie began.

"Yes?"

"We were wondering what the sleeping arrangements are going be when we stop for the night. I mean, you obviously—for some unspecified reason—can't let us out of your sight . . ."

"You sleep in the car. I drive. There'll be no stopping at motorway hotels. This is a one-hop run . . ."

"Very Chinese," Sukie muttered.

". . . and the sooner we get to Salzburg the sooner I can release you. The local police will take charge of things after that."

"What are these *things,* James?" Again from Sukie. "Look, you've explained a little bit. We both think you're a nice guy with some pretty heavy problems. We accept that we're hostages, but we'd like to help . . ."

"I can't trust you—I can't trust anyone," Bond said soberly. "Thanks for the offer, Sukie, but truly you'd be out of your depth. I just want you here in the car until Salzburg."

Nannie spoke up, level-voiced, the tone almost one of admonition: "James, we hardly know each other, but you have to understand that, for us, this is a kind of adventure—something we only read about in books. It's obvious that you're on the side of the angels, unless our intuition's gone right up the spout. This could be routine for you, but it's so abnormal for us that it's exciting."

"We'd better get back to the car," Bond said flatly. "I've already explained to Sukie that it's really about as exciting as being attacked by a swarm of killer bees." Inside, he knew the girls were either going through a form of transference, like hostages starting to identify with their captors, or trying to establish a rapport in order to lull him into complacency. To increase chances of survival he had to remain detached; and that was not an easy option with a pair of young women as attractive and desirable as Sukie and Nannie.

Nannie gave a sigh of exasperation, and Sukie started to say something, but Bond stopped them with a movement of his hand.

"Into the car," he ordered.

They made exceptional time on the long run up through the twisting Malojapass, through St. Moritz, finally crossing into Austria at Vinadi, so that just before seven-thirty in the evening they were cruising at speed along the A12 Autobahn, having skirted Innsbruck, now heading northeast. Within the hour they would turn further east onto the A8, which would lead them to Salzburg. The day had been blazing hot, even high among the mountains, and the girls, when not indulging themselves in the trivial pursuits of their world—which ranged from haute couture to the latest scandals of their particular sets—proved not to be insensible to the rugged and incredible grandeur of the terrain through which they passed.

Bond drove with care and relentless concentration, cursing the situation in which he found himself. So beautiful was the day, so impressive the scenery, that, had things been different, the ever-changing landscape, combined with the two girls, would have made this a memorable holiday indeed.

His eyes searched the road ahead, scanning the traffic, their signals, then swiftly crossing the instruments to check speed, fuel consumption and temperature.

"Remember the silver Renault, James?" Nannie, in an almost teasing voice from the rear. "Well, I think it's behind us, moving up fast."

"Guardian angels," Bond breathed. "The devil take guardian angels."

"The plates are the same," from Sukie. "I remember them from Brissago. But I think the occupants've changed."

Bond glanced into the mirror. Sure enough, a silver Renault 25 was coming up fast, about half a mile behind them. From the mirror he could not make out the passengers. "Might have changed crews," he said. He was calm about it; after all they were only Steve Quinn's people—angered probably by being given the slip, but on guard just the same. "Let them have their day," he said, then touched the brakes and pulled into the far lane, watching from his offside wing mirror.

He was conscious of a tension between the two girls, like game that sensed the hunter. Fear suddenly seemed to flood the interior of the car, almost tangible, a scent of danger.

The road ahead was empty, ribbon straight, with grassland curving upward toward outcrops of rock and the inevitable pine and fir, abundant and thick. Bond's eyes flicked to the wing mirror again, and he glimpsed the hard, screwed-up concentration on the face of the Renault's driver.

The red dropping ball of the sun was behind them, so the silver car was using the old fighter pilot tactic—coming out of the sun. As the Bentley swung for a second, the crimson fire filled the wing mirror. The next moment, Bond was depressing the accelerator, feeling the proximity of death.

The Bentley responded as only that machine can, a surge of power, effortlessly pushing them forward. But he was a fraction late. The Renault was already almost abreast of them and going flat out.

He heard one of the girls shout, and felt a blast of air as a rear window was operated. One hand came off the wheel as he drew the ASP, dropping it into his lap, the hand moving to the row of switches that operated the electric windows. Somehow he realized that Sukie had shouted for them to get down, while Nannie Norrich had lowered her window with the individual switch.

"Onto the floor!" He heard his own voice as a second blast of air began to circulate within the car, his own offside window sliding down to the pressure of his thumb on the switch.

He heard Nannie shout from the rear, yelling, "They're going to shoot," and the distinctive barrel of a pump-action sawn-off Winchester showed, for a split second, from the rear window of the Renault.

Then came the two blasts, one sharp and from behind his right shoulder, filling the car with a film of gray mist bearing the unmistakable smell of cordite. The other was louder, but farther away, almost drowned by the engine noise, the rush of wind into the car and the ringing in his own ears.

The Mulsanne Turbo bucked to the right, as though some giant metal boot-tip had struck the rear with force; the push was accompanied by a rending, clattering noise, like stones hitting them. Then another bang from behind him.

He saw the silver car to their left, almost abreast of them, a haze of smoke being whipped from the rear where someone crouched at the window. The Winchester's barrel was trained on them.

"Down, Sukie!" he shouted, his voice rising to a scream as his own hand came up to fire through the open window—two rounds, precise and aimed toward the driver.

There was a lurching sensation, then a grinding as the sides of the two cars grated together, then drifted apart, followed by another crack from the rear of the Bentley.

They must have been touching 100 kph, and Bond knew he had almost lost control of the big car as it veered and snaked across the road. He pumped the brakes, watched the road now, touched the brakes twice more and felt the speed bleed off as the front wheels mounted the grass verge.

There was a sliding sensation, then a rocking bump as they stopped. "Out!" Bond yelled, "Out! On the far side! Use the car for cover!"

When he reached the relative safety of the car's side, he saw Sukie had followed him and was lying as though trying to push herself into the earth. Nannie, on the other hand, was crouched behind the trunk, her cotton skirt hitched up to show a stocking top and part of a white garter belt. The skirt had hooked itself onto a neat, soft leather holster, on the inside of her thigh, and she held a small .22 pistol very professionally, in a two-handed grip, pointing across the trunk.

"The law would be very angry," Nannie shouted, "they're coming back. Wrong side of the motorway."

"What the hell. . . ?" Bond began.

"Get your gun and shoot at them," Nannie laughed. "Come on, Master James, Nannie knows best."

— 6 —

The NUB

OVER THE LONG SNOUT of the Bentley, Bond saw the truth. He had no time to go into the whys and wherefores of Nannie's professional actions, her gun or how he had missed finding it. The silver Renault was streaking toward them, up the slow lane, moving in the wrong direction, regardless of two other careening cars and a lorry, all three of which weaved and screeched over the wide autobahn to avoid collision.

"The tires," Nannie said coolly. "Go for the tires."

"*You* go for the tires," Bond snapped, angry at being given instructions by the girl. He had his own method of stopping the car, which was now almost on top of them.

In the fraction of time before he fired, a host of things crossed his mind. The Renault had originally contained a two-man team. When the hit had come, there were three of them: one in the back with the Winchester, the driver and a back-up who seemed to be using a high-powered revolver. Somehow the shotgun-wielding killer had disappeared, but the one in the passenger seat now had the Winchester. The driver's side window was open, and in a fanatical act of lunacy, the passenger seemed to be leaning across the driver, to fire the Winchester as they came rapidly closer to the Mulsanne Turbo, which was slewed, like a beached whale, just off the hard shoulder of the road.

Bond looked straight over the Guttersnipe sight on the ASP—three long bright grooves that gave a marksman the perfect aiming coordinates by showing a triangle of yellow when it was on target.

He was on target now: aiming not at the tires but at the petrol tank, for the ASP was loaded with those most horrific projectiles, Glaser Slugs—prefragmented bullets, each containing hundreds of number 12 shot suspended in liquid Teflon. The effect of an impact from just one of these appalling little bullets was devastating, for the projectile would penetrate skin, bone, tissue or metal, before almost literally exploding the mass of tiny steel balls. They would cut a man in half at a few paces, take out a leg or arm and certainly ignite petrol in a vehicle's tank.

Bond began to take up the first pressure on the trigger, and, as the rear of the Renault came fully into the triangle of his sights, he squeezed hard. As he got the two shots away he was conscious of the double crack from his left—Nannie giving the tires hell.

Several things happened quickly. The nearside front tire crossed the great divide in a terrible burning and shredding of rubber—Bond remembered thinking that she had been very lucky to get a couple of puny .22 shots close to the inner section of the tire. The car began to slew inward, toppling slightly, looking as though it would cartwheel straight into the Bentley, but the driver struggled with wheel and brakes, and the silver car just about stayed in line, hopelessly doomed, but running fast and straight toward the hard shoulder.

This all happened in a millisecond, for, as the tire disintegrated, so the two Glaser Slugs from the ASP scorched through the bodywork and into the petrol tank.

Almost in slow motion, the Renault seemed to continue on its squealing, tippling way. The effect of the Glasers appeared to take minutes, but it happened just as the car had passed the rear of the Bentley—a long, thin sheet of flame, like natural gas being burned off, hissing from the rear of the car. There was even time to notice that the flame was tinged with blue before the whole rear end of the Renault became a rumbling, irregular, boiling, growing crimson ball.

The car now began its cartwheel, and was, in fact,

a burning, twisted wreck—a hundred yards or so to the rear of the Bentley—by the time the noise reached them: a great hiss and whump, followed by a screaming of rubber and metal as the vehicle went through its spectacular death throes.

Nobody moved for a second. Then Bond reacted. Two or three cars were approaching the scene, and he was in no mood to be involved with the police at this stage.

"What kind of shape are we in?" he called.

"Dented, a lot of holes in the bodywork, but the wheels seem okay." Nannie was at the other side of the car. She unhitched her skirt from the garter belt, showing a fragment of white lace as she did so. "There's a very nasty scrape down this side. Stem to stern."

Bond looked towards Sukie, asking if she was okay. "Shaken, but undamaged, I think."

"In!" Bond commanded crisply. "Into the car. Both of you," as he dived toward the driving seat, conscious of at least one car, containing people in checked shirts, floppy hats and the usual impediments of tourists, drawing up cautiously to the rear of the burning wreckage.

He twisted the key, almost viciously, in the ignition. The huge engine throbbed into life immediately, and, without ceremony, he knocked off the main brake with his left hand, slid into drive and smoothly gunned the Mulsanne Turbo back onto the motorway.

The traffic remained sparse, giving Bond the opportunity to run through checks on the car's engine and handling. There was no loss of fuel, oil or hydraulic pressure; he went steadily up the steps, through the gears and back again. Brakes appeared unaffected. The cruise control went in and came out normally, while whatever damage had been done to the body did not appear to have affected either suspension or handling.

After five minutes he was satisfied the car was relatively undamaged. There was, he did not doubt, a good deal of penetration from the couple of Winchester blasts.

The car, with its damage, would now be a sitting target for the Austrian police who, like the forces of most Western countries, were not enamored of shoot-outs between cars on their relatively safe autobahns—particularly when one of the vehicles, and its occupants, ends up incinerated.

There was need to reach a telephone quite quickly, alert London and get them to call the Austrian dogs off. Bond was also concerned about the possible fate of Steve Quinn's team.

Something else nagged at his mind. Nannie Norrich swam, an image, into his head—the lush thigh, and the .22 pistol being expertly handled.

"I think you'd better let me have the armory, Nannie," he said quietly, hardly turning his head.

"Oh, no, James. No, James. No," she sang, quite prettily.

"I don't like women roving around with guns, especially in the current situation, and within this car. How in heaven's name did I miss it anyway?"

"Because, while you're obviously a pro, you're also a bit of a gent, James. You failed to grope the inside of my thighs when you frisked me in Cannobio."

He recalled her flirtatious manner, and the cheeky smile. "So, I suppose I now pay for the error. Are you going to tell me it's pointing at the back of my head?"

"Actually it's pointing toward my own left knee, back where it belongs. Not the most comfortable place to have a weapon." She paused. "Well, not *that* kind of weapon anyway."

A sign came up indicating a picnic area, ahead and to their right. Bond slowed, pulling off the road, down a track through dense fir trees and into a clearing. Rustic tables and benches stood in the center of the clearing. There was not a picnicker in sight.

To one side—praise heaven—a neat, clean and unvandalized telephone booth awaited them.

Bond brought the car to a halt in the shade of the trees, turning it so that they could make a quick exit if necessary. He cut the engine, clicked off his seatbelt and turned to face Nannie Norrich, holding out his

88

right hand, palm upward. "The gun, Nannie. I have to make a couple of important calls, and I'm in enough danger already. Just give me the gun."

Nannie smiled at him, a gentle, fond smile. "You'd have to take it from me, James, and that might not be as easy as you imagine. Look, I used that weapon to help *you*. Sukie's given me my orders. I *am* to cooperate—to assist—and I can assure you that, had she instructed otherwise, you would have known it within a very short time of my joining you in the car."

"*Sukie's* ordered you?" Bond felt lost.

"She's my boss. For the time being anyway. I take orders from her, and . . ."

Sukie Tempesta put a hand on Bond's arm. "I think I should explain, James. Nannie *is* an old school friend. She is also president of NUB."

"And what the devil's the NUB?" Bond was cross now.

"Norrich Universal Bodyguards."

"What?"

"Minders," said Nannie, still very cheerful.

"Minders?" For a second he was incredulous.

"Minders, as in people who look after other people for money. Minders. Protectors. Heavies." Nannie began again. "James, NUB is an all-women outfit. Staffed by a special kind of woman. My girls are exceptionally trained—weaponry, karate, all the martial arts, driving, flying, you name it, we do it. Truly, we're good, and with an exceptional clientele."

"And the Principessa Sukie Tempesta is among that clientele?"

"Naturally. I try to do that particular job myself whenever possible."

"Your people didn't do it very well the other evening in Belgium," Bond said sharply. "At the filling station. I ought to charge commission."

Nannie sighed, "It *was* unfortunate . . ."

"It was also my fault," added Sukie. "Nannie wanted to pick me up in Brussels, when her deputy had to leave. I said I'd make it without any problems. I was wrong."

"Of course you were wrong. Look, James, you've got problems. So has Sukie, mainly because she's a multimillionaire who insists on living in Rome for most of the year—and that's damned dangerous. Kidnappings of the wealthy are daily happenings, so she's a sitting duck. Now, you go and make your telephone calls. Just trust me. Trust us. Trust NUB."

Eventually Bond shrugged, took the keys out of the ignition, and climbed from the car, locking the two girls in behind him.

After retrieving the CC500 from the trunk, he went over to the telephone booth, made the slightly more complex attachments needed for pay phones and dialed the operator, placing a call to the Resident's number in Vienna.

The conversation was short and to the point, ending with the Resident agreeing to fix the Austrian police, and even arranging for a patrol to come out to where he was parked—if possible with the senior officer in charge of the May/Moneypenny kidnapping. "Sit tight," he counseled. "They should be with you in an hour or so."

Bond hung up, redialed the operator and within seconds was speaking to the duty officer at the Regent's Park HQ in London.

"Rome's two men are dead," the officer told him, without emotion. "Found shot through the back of the head in a ditch. Stay on the line, M wants a word."

A moment later his Chief's voice sounded, gruff, in his ear. "Bad business, James." M only called him James in moments of great stress.

"*Very* bad, sir. Moneypenny as well as my housekeeper."

"Yes, and whoever has them is trying to strike a hard bargain."

"Sir?"

"Nobody's told you?"

"I haven't seen anyone to speak to, sir."

There was a long pause. Then, "The women will be returned, unharmed, within forty-eight hours in exchange for you."

"Ah," said Bond, "I thought it might be something like that. The Austrian police know of this?"

"I gather they have some details."

"Then I'll hear it all when they arrive. I understand they're on their way. Please tell Rome I'm sorry about his two boys."

"Take care, 007. We don't give in to terrorist demands in the Service. You know that policy, and you must abide by it. No heroics. No throwing your life away. You are not, repeat *not* to comply."

"There might be no other way, sir."

"There's always another way. Find it; and find it soon." He closed the line.

Bond unhooked the CC500. Already he knew that his life was possibly forfeit for those of May and Moneypenny. If there *was* no other way, then he would have to die. He also knew that he would go on to the bitter end, taking risks, but in the last resort . . . well, they would have to see. Slowly he walked back to the car.

It took exactly one hour and thirty-six minutes for the two police cars to arrive: just time enough for Bond to hear how Nannie, always good at sports, in spite of what she called "my odd eyeballs," had put her natural talents to good use by founding the thriving Norrich Universal Bodygurds—"The nub of the matter," as she said.

In five years she had established branches in London, Paris, Rome, Los Angeles and New York, yet never once had she advertized the service. "If I did, there would be people who'd imagine we were call girls. It's been a word-of-mouth thing from the start. What's more, it's fun."

Bond wondered why he, or his Service, had never heard of them. NUB appeared to be an excellently kept secret, operating within the enclosed confines of the ultra-rich. "We don't usually get spotted," she told him. "Men out with a girl minder look as though they're merely on a date, and when I go to some function with somebody like Sukie we always make certain we both have safe men with us." She laughed. "I've seen poor Sukie through two dramatic love affairs in the last year alone."

Sukie opened her mouth in apparent retort to Nannie's remark, but at that moment, the police arrived—two cars, unheralded by klaxons, sweeping into the glade in a cloud of dust.

There were four uniformed officers in the second car and three in the first, plus another in civilian clothes. The plainclothed man unfolded himself from the rear of the first car and stretched, as though sitting in the vehicle had done terrible things to his long bones.

He was immensely tall but immaculately dressed. The latter was necessary, for his whole frame was built out of proportion and only an expert tailor could possibly make him even half presentable. His arms were long, ending with very small hands that seemed to hang almost down to his knees, like an ape's, while his face, crowned with a gleaming full head of hair, was too large for the oddly thin shoulders.

He had the apple cheeks of a fat farmer and large horn-rimmed spectacles that gave him an owlish look, while a pair of great jug-handle ears made the head almost aerodynamic. The man could be taken for a freak, a walking joke.

"Oh, my God," Nannie's whisper filled the interior of the car with a shiver of fear. "Put your hands in sight. Let them see your hands." It was something Bond had already done instinctively.

"Der Haken!" Nannie whispered again.

"The hook?" Bond hardly moved his lips as he queried her German.

"Real name's Inspector Heinrich Osten. Well over retirement age and stuck as an inspector, but he's the most ruthless, corrupt bastard in Austria." She still whispered, as though the man, who had now started to shamble toward the Bentley, could hear every word. "They say nobody's ever dared ask for his retirement because he literally knows where all the bodies're buried."

"He knows you?" Bond asked.

"Never met him. But he's on our files. The story is that as a very, *very,* young man he was an ardent National Socialist. They call him Der Haken because he favored a butcher's hook as a torture implement. If we're dealing with this joker, James, don't trust him, don't believe him and, for God's sake, don't be taken in by him."

Inspector Osten had reached the Bentley, and now stood, backed by two uniformed men, on Bond's side of the car. He stooped, as though folding his body straight from the waist—Bond had the mental picture of an oil pump—and waggled his small fingers outside the driver's window. The fingers rippled, as though he was trying to attract the attention of a baby.

Bond activated the window.

"Herr Bond?" The voice was high-pitched, low in volume.

"Yes. Bond. James Bond."

"Good. We are to give you protection to Salzburg. Please to get out of your car for a moment."

Bond opened the door, climbed out and looked up at the beaming, polished-apple cheeks, and grasped the obscenely small hand, outstretched in greeting. It was like touching the dry skin of a snake.

"I am in charge of the case, Herr Bond. The case of the missing ladies—a good mystery title, *ja?*"

There was silence. Bond was not prepared to laugh at May's or Moneypenny's predicament.

"So," the inspector became serious again. "I am pleased to meet you. My name is Osten. Heinrich Osten." His mouth opened in a grimace that revealed blackened teeth. "Some people like to call me by another name. Der Haken. I do not know why, but it sticks. Probably it is because I hook out criminals." He laughed again. "I think, perhaps, I might even have hooked you, Herr Bond. The two of us have much to talk about. A great deal. I think I shall ride in your motor so we can talk. The ladies can go in the other cars."

95

"No!" Nannie objected violently.

"Oh, but yes." Osten reached for the rear door and tugged it open.

Already a uniformed man was half helping and half dragging Sukie from the passenger side.

The girls went, kicking and screaming, to the other cars. Bond hoped Nannie had the sense not to reveal, or use, the .22.

Osten gave his apple smile again. "We shall talk better without the tattle of women, I think. In any case, Herr Bond, you do not wish them to hear me charge you with being an accessory to kidnapping and, possibly, murder, do you?"

— 7 —

The Hook

BOND DROVE WITH EXAGGERATED CARE. For one thing, the man who now sat next to him gave off incredibly sinister vibrations of danger. It was like being close to an unstable bomb. The grotesque Inspector Osten had about him an aura of sweating gelignite, mixed with an odd sensation of latent insanity. Bond had felt the presence of evil many times in his life, but now it was as strong as he could ever recall.

Osten smelled of something else, and it took time to identify the old-fashioned bay rum that he obviously used in large quantities on his thatch of hair.

They were several kilometers along the road before the silence was broken. "Murder and kidnapping," Osten said quietly, almost to himself.

"Blood sports," Bond answered placidly, and the policeman gave a low rumbling chuckle.

"Blood sports is good, Mr. Bond. Very good."

"And you're going to charge me with them?"

Once more the laugh. "I can have you for murder. You and the two young women. How do you say in England? On toast, I can have you."

"I think you should check with your superiors before you try anything like that. In particular your own Security and Intelligence Department."

Osten gave a short, rough, contemptuous laugh. "Those skulking, prying idiots have little jurisdiction over me, Mr. Bond . . ."

"You're a law unto yourself, Inspector?"

There was a slow sigh, which seemed to go on for a long time. Then, "In this instance I *am* the law, and that's what matters. You have been concerned for two English ladies who have disappeared from a clinic . . ."

"One is a Scottish lady, Inspector."

"Whatever." He raised a tiny hand, like that of a doll, grafted onto the long stump of arm, an action at once dismissive and full of derision. "You are the only outside key; the linking factor in this small mystery; the man who knew both victims. It is natural, then, that I must question you—interrogate you—thoroughly regarding these disappearances . . ."

"I've yet to learn the details myself. One of the ladies is my housekeeper."

98

"The younger one?" The question was asked in a particularly unpleasant manner, and Bond replied with some vehemence.

"No, Inspector, the elderly Scottish lady. She's been with me for many years. The younger lady is a colleague, and I think you should forget about interrogations until you hear from people of slightly higher status than yourself."

"There are other questions—bringing a firearm into the country, a public shoot-out that caused not only the deaths of three men, but also great danger to innocent people using the autobahn."

"With respect, the three men were trying to kill *me*, and the two ladies who were in my car."

Osten nodded, but it was a gesture that contained reservations. "We shall see. In Salzburg we shall see." Casually, the man they called the Hook leaned over, his long arm stabbing forward, like a reptile, the tiny hand moving like a rock crab. The inspector was more than just very experienced, Bond thought, he also had a highly developed intuition, for, within seconds, the little hands had removed both the ASP and the baton from their respective holsters.

"I am always uncomfortable with a man armed like this." The apple cheeks puffed, like a balloon blowing up, into a red, shiny smile.

"If you take my wallet, you'll find that I have an international licence to carry the gun." Bond sat, grim, behind the wheel.

"We shall see." Osten gave another sigh, repeating, "In Salzburg we shall see."

It was late when they reached the city, and Osten began to give him terse instructions—a left here, then a right and another right. Bond caught a glimpse of the River Salzach, the bridges and, behind him, the old town, with the Hohensalzburg castle—once the stronghold of the prince-archbishops—standing, floodlit on its great lump of dolomite rock, above the town and river.

They were heading for the new town, which was no surprise, and Bond quite expected to be guided towards police headquarters. Instead, he found himself driving through a maze of streets, past a pair of very modern apartment blocks and down into an underground car park.

The other two cars, which they appeared to have lost on the outskirts of the city, waited, parked neatly with a space between them for the Bentley. The police were still sitting in their vehicles, and the girls had been separated, one to each car.

An uneasy sensation, like a facial tic, flashed through Bond's nervous system. He had been assured by the Resident that the police were there to get him safely into Salzburg. Now, he was faced not only with a very unpleasant and probably corrupt policeman, but also with what was obviously some plan to bring him, and the girls, into a possibly unofficial building—for he had no doubt that the car park belonged

100

to the second of the modern blocks of luxury apartments.

"Lower my window," Osten spoke quietly. One of the policemen had come over to the passenger side of the Bentley, and another stood forward of the vehicle. The second man had a machine pistol tucked into his hip, the evil eye of the muzzle pointing directly at Bond.

Now, through the open window, Der Haken muttered a few rapid, commanding sentences in German to the officer beside the car. His voice was pitched so low, and his German, tinged with that odd high-piping Viennese accent, was so rapid that Bond caught only a few words—"The women first," then a mutter, "separate rooms . . . under guard at all times . . . until we have everything sorted out . . ." He ended with a question, which Bond did not catch at all. The answer, however, was clear.

"You are to telephone him as soon as possible."

Heinrich Osten nodded, the oversized head like that of a souvenir doll designed to sit in the rear of a car window. He told the uniformed man to carry on. The one with the machine pistol did not move.

"We sit, quietly, for a few minutes." The head turned, red cheeks puffed in a smile.

"I think, as you have only hinted at possible charges against me, I should be allowed to speak to my embassy in Vienna." Bond clipped out the words, as though they were parade ground orders.

101

"All in good time. There are formalities." Osten was terrifyingly calm, sitting with hands folded, as one who has complete command of the situation.

"Formalities? What *formalities*?" Bond shouted. "People have rights. In particular, I am on an official assignment. I demand to—"

Osten gave the hint of a nod toward the machine-pistol-toting policeman, "You can demand nothing, Mr. Bond. Surely you understand that. You are a stranger in a strange land. By the very fact that I am the law—and you have an Uzi trained on you—your rights are forfeit. No demands can be met."

He saw the two girls being hustled from the other cars. They were kept well apart and both looked considerably frightened. Sukie did not even turn her head in the direction of the Bentley, but Nannie glanced toward him. In a fragment of time the message was clear in her eyes. She was still armed and biding her time. A remarkably tough lady, he thought: tough, and attractive in a scrubbed kind of way, for—on purpose, he presumed—she made no concession to glamor, with the granny glasses and no-nonsense hair.

The women disappeared from Bond's line of vision, and a moment later Osten prodded him in the ribs, with his own ASP. "Leave the keys in the car, Mr. Bond. It has to be moved from here before the morning. Just get out, showing your hands the whole time. My officer with the Uzi is a little nervous."

Bond did as he was bidden. It felt quite cool in the almost bare underground park—eerie and smelling, like all car parks, of gasoline, rubber and oil.

The man with the machine pistol motioned to him to walk between the other cars, through a small exit passage and toward what appeared to be a brick wall. Osten made a slight movement, and Bond caught sight of a flat remote controller in his left hand. Without even a click, a door-sized section of the brickwork moved silently inward, and then slid to one side, revealing steel elevator doors. Somewhere, far away in the car park, an engine fired, throbbed and settled as a vehicle made its exit.

The elevator arrived with a brief sigh, and Bond was signaled to enter. The three men stood, silent, as the lift cage made its noiseless upward journey. The doors slid open and, again, Bond was ushered forward, this time into a passageway, lined with modern prints, a thick pile carpet underfoot. A second later they were in a large apartment of obvious luxury and impeccable taste.

The carpets were Turkish, and of value; the furnishings modern, but obviously custom-built—wood, steel, glass and expensive fabrics—while the walls sported paintings and drawings by Piper, Sutherland, Bonnard, Gross and Hockney. The entrance passage led to a large, open room, with great glass windows, firmly shut, but disclosing a wide balcony. To the left an archway revealed the dining area and kitchen, while two other, lower arches faced them showing only long passages studded with gleaming white doors. A police officer stood in each of the passages, as though on guard.

Through the huge glass windows, you could just glimpse the floodlit Hohensalzburg, and Osten must have seen Bond's head turn to look, for he quickly commanded that the curtains be closed. Light blue velvet slid electronically on soundless rails.

"Nice little place you have, for a police inspector," Bond said.

"Ah, my friend. Would it were mine. I have only borrowed it for this one evening."

Bond nodded, trying to indicate this was obvious, if only because of the style and elegance. He turned to face the inspector, and began speaking rapidly, "Now, sir. I appreciate what you've told me, but you must know that the embassy, and officers of the department I represent, have already given instructions, and received assurances from your own people. You say I have no right to demand anything, but you make a grave error there. In fact I have the right to demand everything."

Der Haken looked at him glassy-eyed, then gave a distinct chuckle. "If you were alive, Mr. Bond. Yes, if you were still alive you would have the right; while I would have the duty to cooperate if I were also alive. Unhappily we are both dead men."

Bond scowled, puzzled, though the first glimmer of truth was starting to force itself into his head.

"The problem is actually yours," the policeman continued, "for you *really* are a dead man."

Osten, smiling, glanced around him. "I shall be living in this kind of world very shortly. A good place for a ghost, yes?"

"Enchanting; and what kind of place will I be haunting?"

Any trace of humanity disappeared from the policeman's face. The muscles turned to hard rock, and the glassy eyes broke and splintered. Even the apple cheeks seemed to lose color and become sallow. "The grave, Mr. Bond. You will be haunting the cold, cold grave. You will be nowhere. Nothing. It will be as though you had never existed." His small hand flicked up so that he could glance at his wristwatch, and he turned to the man with the Uzi, sharply ordering him to turn on the television. "The late news will be starting any moment." Still no humor. "My death should already have been reported. Yours will be announced as probable—though it will be more than probable before dawn. Please sit down and watch. I think you'll agree that my improvisation has been brilliant, for I had only a very short time to set things up."

Bond slumped into a chair, half his mind on the chances of dealing with the policeman and his accomplices, the other half working out what had been planned and why.

There were commercials on the big color screen. Attractive Austrian girls stood against mountain scenery and told the world of the essential value of a sun barrier cream; a young man arrived, hatless, from the air, climbed from his light aircraft cockpit and said the view was *wunderschön* but even more *wunderschön* when you used a certain kind of camera to capture it; while a badly dubbed American advertisement extolled the value of a preparation for hemorrhoids.

The news graphics filled the screen, and a serious brunette appeared. The lead story was about a shooting and tragedy on the A8 autobahan. One car, carrying seemingly innocent tourists, had been fired at and crashed in flames—the pictures showed the recognizable wreckage of the silver Renault, surrounded by police and ambulances. The young woman, now looking very grave, appeared again to say that the horror had been compounded by the death of five police officers in a freak accident as they sped from Salzburg to the scene of the shooting. One of the police cars had gone out of control, and was hit, broadside on, by the other. Both cars had skidded into woodland and caught fire.

There was another series of pictures showing the remains of the two cars. Then Inspector Heinrich Osten's official photograph came up in black and white, and the newsperson informed Austria that the country had lost one of its most efficient and long-serving officers in this disaster. The inspector had been traveling in the second car, and his body, like those of his companions, was incinerated beyond identification.

Next, Bond saw his own photograph, and the number plate of the Bentley Mulsanne Turbo. He was a British diplomat, traveling on private business, probably with two young women—unidentified—and was wanted for questioning regarding the original shoot-out. A statement from the embassy said he had telephoned appealing for help, but they feared he might have been affected by stress and run amok. "He has been under great strain during the last few days," a bland embassy spokesman told a television reporter. So the Service and Foreign Office had decided to deny him. Well, that was standard. The car, diplomat and young women had disappeared, and there were fears for their lives. Police would resume the search at daybreak, but the car could easily have gone off one of the mountain roads. The worst was expected.

Der Haken began to laugh. "You see how simple it all is, Mr. Bond? When they find your car, smashed to pieces at the bottom of a ravine—probably sometime tomorrow—the search will be over. There will be three mutilated bodies inside."

The full impact of the inspector's plan had struck home. "And mine will be minus its head, I presume?" Bond asked calmly.

"Naturally." He scowled. "It would appear that you know what's going on."

"I know that, somehow, you've managed to murder five of your colleagues . . ."

The tiny hand came up. "No! No! Not my colleagues, Mr. Bond. Tramps, vagrants. Scum. Yes, we put an end to some scum—"

"With two extra police cars?"

"With the two original police cars. The ones down in the garage are the fakes. We have kept a pair of white VWs, complete with detachable police decals and plates, for a long while, on the off chance that the time would come when I might need them. The moment arrived suddenly."

"Yesterday?"

"When I discovered the true reason for the kidnapping of your friends—and the reward. Yesterday. I have means. Ways and means to contact people. Once the ransom demand was clear I made inquiries, and came up with . . ."

"The Head Hunt."

"Precisely. You're very well informed. Those who are offering the very large prize for what appears to be the second-most-important piece of your anatomy gave me the impression that you were in the dark— that is correct? In the dark?"

Bond nodded. "For a late starter, Inspector, you seem to be well organized," he said.

"Ach! Organized!" The polished cheeks blossomed with unpleasant pride. "When you have spent most of your life being ready to move at short notice, you make certain you are ready to go, and have ways, means, papers, friends, transport."

108

Obviously the man was very sure of himself, as well he might be with Bond caught in a building high above Salzburg, which had been his territory for a long time. He was also expansive. "I always knew the moment for wealth and personal escape would come through something like a blackmail or kidnapping case. The petty criminals could never supply me with the kind of money I really need to be independent. If I was able to do a private deal, in, as I have said, a blackmail or kidnapping case, then my last years were secure. Though never, even in my craziest dreams, did I expect the luck and riches that have come with you, Herr Bond." He beamed, like a malicious and evil child. "In my time here I have made sure that my personal team had the correct incentives. Now they have a great and always good reason for helping me and moving with me. They're not really uniformed men, of course. They are my squad of detectives. But they would die for me . . ."

"Or for the money," Bond said coldly. "They might even dispose of *you* for the money."

Der Haken growled a laugh. "You have to be up early in the morning to catch an old bird like me, Herr Bond. They could try to kill me, I suppose, but I doubt it. What I do not doubt is that they will help me to dispose of you." He rose. "You will excuse me, I have an important telephone call to make."

Bond lifted a hand. "Inspector! One favor! The girls are here?"

"Naturally."

"They have nothing to do with me. A chance meeting. They're uninvolved, so I ask you to let them go."

Der Haken did not even look at him, muttering, "Impossible," as he strode off down one of the passageways.

The man with the Uzi smiled at Bond over the barrel, then spoke in bad English, "He is very clever, Der Haken, yes? Always he promised us that, one day, there would be a way to make us all rich. Now he says we shall all be sitting in sunshine and luxury soon. There will be women." His smile turned into a leer, and Bond thought how easy it was to manipulate men with the glint of fairy gold. Like as not, Osten would see his four accomplices at the bottom of some ravine before he made off with the reward—if he ever got the reward. In German, he asked the Uzi-holder how they had concocted a plan so quickly.

It appeared that they had been working on the kidnapping at the Klinik Mozart. There were various telephone calls. Suddenly the inspector disappeared for about an hour. On his return he was jubilant. He had brought them all to this apartment and explained the situation. All they had to do was catch a man called Bond. Once they had him, the kidnapping would be over—only there was a bonus. The people who owned this very apartment would see the women

110

returned to the Klinik *and* provide a huge amount of money for Herr Bond's head.

"The inspector kept calling in to headquarters," the man told him. "He was trying to find out where you were. When he discovered, we left in the cars. We were already on the way when the radio call told us you were waiting off the A8. There had been shooting and a car was destroyed. He thinks on his feet, the inspector. We picked up five vagrants, from the worst area of the town, and drove them to the place where we keep the other cars. The rest was easy. We had uniforms with the cars; the vagrants were drunk, and easy to make completely unconscious. The accident was simple to stage. Then we came on to pick you up." He was not certain of the next moves in the game but knew his chief would get the money; and, at that moment, Der Haken returned.

"It is all arranged," he smiled. "I fear I shall have to lock you in one of the rooms, like the girls, Herr Bond. But only for an hour or two. I have a visitor. When my visitor has gone we will all go for a short drive into the mountains. The Head Hunt is almost over."

Bond nodded, thinking to himself that the Head Hunt was *not* almost over. There were always ways. He now had to find a way—and quickly—to get himself and the girls out of Der Haken's clutches. The grotesque Inspector Osten was gesturing with the ASP, indicating that Bond should head down the righthand passageway.

Bond took a step toward the arch, then stopped. "Two questions—last requests, if you like . . ."

"The women have to go," Osten said quietly. "I cannot keep witnesses."

"And I would do the same in your shoes. I understand. No, my questions are merely to ease my own mind. First, who were the men in the Renault—they were obviously taking part in this bizarre hunt for my head? I'd like to know."

"Union Corse, so I understand." Der Haken was in a hurry, agitated, as though his visitor would arrive at any moment.

"And what exactly happened to my housekeeper and Miss Moneypenny?"

"Happened? They were kidnapped."

"Yes, but the events. How did it take place?"

The policeman gave an irritated snarl, "I haven't got time to go into details now. They were kidnapped. You do not need to know anything else." He gave Bond a light push, heading him in the direction of the passage.

They came to a door—third on the right. Osten unlocked it, and almost threw Bond inside. He heard the key turn and the lock thud home.

It was a guest bedroom: bright, with a single modern four-poster, more expensive prints, an armchair, dressing table and built-in wardrobe. The single window was draped with heavy and expensive cream curtains.

He moved quickly, first checking the window. He appeared to be at the side of the building, and thought the long balcony off the main room probably ran around the angle of the wall, for the casement window looked out on to a narrow section of balcony—almost certainly an offshoot of the large main terrace. The window glass was thick and unbreakable. The locks were high-security, and while not completely beyond him, would take time to remove. Already he realized an assault on the door was out of the question. The lock had been Chubb—a deadlock—not easy to manipulate without a great deal of noise, and the only tools hidden on him were small. At a pinch he might just do the window, but what then? He was at least six stories above ground, unarmed, and without any aids to assist a climb down a well-lit apartment block.

He checked the wardrobe, which, like every drawer in the place, was empty. As he did so, a series of sharp rings came from far away in the main area of the flat. The visitor had arrived—Tamil Rahani's emissary, he supposed, certainly someone of authority within SPECTRE. Time was running out, so it would have to be the window.

Oddly, for a policeman, Osten had left him with his belt. Thank heaven, for there, sewn carefully, and almost undetectably, between the thick leather strips was a long, thin multipurpose tool, built like a very slim Swiss Army knife. Fashioned in toughened steel, it contained a whole set of miniature tools ranging from screwdrivers and picklocks to a tiny battery and connectors that could, in emergency, be used in conjunction with three small explosive charges, the size and thickness of a fingernail, hidden in the casing.

The Toolkit had been designed by the Armorer's—Major Boothroyd's—brilliant assistant in Q Branch, Anne Reilly, known to all within the Regent's Park Headquarters as Q'ute. Now Bond silently blessed her ingenuity as he set to work on the security locks, which were screwed tightly into the metal frame of the casement.

There were two, plus the actual lock on the window handle, and the first took a good ten minutes to remove. At this rate he had at least another twenty minutes' work—possibly more—and he guessed that kind of time was not at his disposal.

He worked on, blistering and grazing his fingers, knowing the alternative—trying to blow out the Chubb deadlock on the door—was of no value, for they would cut him down almost before he could reach the passage.

From time to time he stopped, standing to listen for any noise that might indicate action from within the apartment. Not a sound reached him, and he finally disposed of the second lock. All that remained was the main window catch, and he had just started to work on it when a blaze of light came on outside. Somebody in the main room had switched on the terrace balcony lights, one of which, he now saw, was bracketed to the wall just outside this particular window.

He still could hear nothing—the place probably had some soundproofing in the walls, while the windows were so toughened and thick that little exterior noise would seep through. After a few seconds, his eyes adjusted to the new light, and he was able to continue his attack on the main lock. Five minutes passed and he only managed to get one screw away. He stopped, leaned against the wall and decided to have a go at the lock mechanism itself, which held down the catch and handle that would at least lead him to the freedom of the balcony.

He tried three different picklocks before hitting on the right one. There was a sharp click as the bar was withdrawn, and a glance at his Rolex told him the whole business had, incredibly, taken over forty-five minutes. There could be very little time left, and he had no firm plan in mind once he reached the terrace.

Quietly, Bond lifted the handle and pulled the window in toward him. There was no squeak, as the hinges were obviously well-oiled, and he was able to draw the small, doorlike window noiselessly into the room. A chill blast of air hit him, and Bond took several deep breaths to clear his head as he stood, ears straining for any sound that might come from the well-lit terrace out of sight, around the corner to his right.

Silence.

The whole thing was odd. Time must now really be trickling out for Der Haken, the crooked police officer who had somehow managed to become a late entrant for this macabre chase, the object of which was, literally, Bond's own head.

It had long been obvious that one of the competitors was looking out for himself, watching, lurking and waiting for the moment to strike—carefully taking out the opposition as he went along. But Der Haken had arrived, unexpectedly, on the scene and, almost certainly, with an offer SPECTRE's leader, Rahani, could not refuse. Among the professional terrorist, criminal and espionage organizations, Osten was the wild card, the joker—the outsider who had suddenly solved SPECTRE's problems.

Carefully, making no noise, Bond eased his way through the window and pressed against the wall. Still no sound. Carefully, he peered around the angle to view the wide terrace, high above Salzburg—a terrace complete with lamps, flowers and white-painted garden furniture. Even Bond took in a quick, startled breath as he looked at the scene.

The lamps were lit, the panorama of the new and old towns twinkled as a beautiful backdrop. The furniture was neatly positioned—as were the bodies.

116

Der Haken's four accomplices had been laid out in a row between the white wrought-iron chairs, each man with the top of his head blown away—the blood stippling the furnishings and walls, seeping out over the flagstones set into the thick concrete balcony.

The long series of windows leading into the main room had been opened, and above them huge pots of geraniums hung, scarlet, on hooks embedded in the wall. One of the pots had been removed. In its place hung a rope, which ended in a reinforced small loop. To the loop, a long, sharp butcher's hook was attached, and from the great spike of the hook, Der Haken himself had been hung.

Bond wondered when he had last witnessed a sight as revolting as this. The policeman's hands and feet were tied together, while the point of the hook had been inserted into his throat. It was long enough to have penetrated through the roof of the mouth, to exit straight through the left eye. Someone had taken great trouble to see that the big, gangling and ungainly man had suffered slowly and unmercifully. If the old Nazi stories were true, then whoever had done this knew Inspector Heinrich Osten's death to be poetic justice.

The body, still dripping blood, swung slightly in the breeze, the neck almost visibly stretching as it moved, and what was left of the face contorted in horrible agony.

Bond swallowed and stepped toward the window.

As he did so, there came a strange, dramatic background sound, mingling with the creak of rope on hook. From across the street, a group of rehearsing musicians began to play. Mozart, naturally—Bond thought it was the somber opening of Piano Concerto no. 20, but his knowledge of Mozart was limited. At the same moment, from further down the street, came the sound of an experienced jazz trumpeter—a busker probably, playing as though shaking his musical fist at the godlike composition of the great Mozart.

It was an odd counterpoint—the precise notes of a Mozart concerto mingling with the old 1930s "Big House Blues." Bond wondered is this was mere coincidence.

— 8 —

Under Discipline

BOND NEEDED TIME TO THINK, but standing on the terrace, in the midst of the carnage, was not the best way to concentrate. It was now three o'clock in the morning and, apart from the music floating from below, the city of Salzburg was silent—a glitter of lights, with the outline of mountains showing pitch black against the dark navy sky.

He walked back into the main room. The lights were still on and there was no sign of any struggle. Whoever had blown way Der Haken and his crew must have operated very quickly. There had to have been more than one of them to deal with five men at speed; also, whoever had done it needed to be known and trusted, at least by Osten. The weapons, it went without saying, must have been silenced.

As his thoughts centered on weapons he realized

there were signs of the violent deaths—traces of blood on the wall between the two archways, and more patches on the deep-pile cream carpet. Also, there, in plain sight on one of the tables, was his ASP and the baton. Bond checked the weapon, which was still loaded and unfired, before returning it to the holster. He paused, weighing the baton for a moment before slipping it into the cylindrical holder still attached to his belt.

Then he went over and closed the windows—Der Haken's body bumping heavily against the glass—and found the button that operated the curtains, blotting out the gruesome sight on the terrace.

He had moved from the balcony with some speed, being very conscious that whoever had put the police officers into permanent sleep could still be in the apartment. Drawing the ASP, Bond now began a systematic search. The apartment appeared to be empty, but for three of the rooms, the doors of which were firmly locked. One was the guest room he had recently vacated; the other two, he reasoned, probably contained Sukie and Nannie. There was no response from either of them when he knocked, and certainly no sign of keys.

His first duty was, naturally, to release the girls—if, indeed, they were there—but he also needed some direction. As he had thought earlier, somebody—one of the Head Hunt competitors—was playing a careful and devious game. Any other competitor who came near to the prize was being eliminated: first the German on the Belgian motorway; then the Poison Dwarf; then the three men killed in the Renault, whom Der Haken had identified as Union Corse. All were criminals, and now the amateur—the rogue policeman—had been taken out, together with his assistants.

Two things worried Bond. Why, when their quarry—himself—was on toast, here in this flat, had they not used the opportunity and killed him on the spot? Second, who were the most likely people to be running this kind of interference? The obvious choice was SPECTRE itself, of course, for it would be their style to mount a competitive kind of operation, with a fabulous price on the victim's head, and then monitor results in order to step in at the last moment. That was the way to save money: to have your cake and eat it.

But, if SPECTRE was responsible for knocking out the opposition, they would certainly have disposed of him by now, so who was left? Possibly one of the unsympathetic espionage organizations that were natural entrants—the first choice among these would, naturally, be the current successors to Bond's old enemy SMERSH.

Since he had first encountered this black and devious arm of the KGB, SMERSH—an acronym for *Smiert Shpionam*, Death to Spies—had undergone a whole series of changes within the constantly altering structure of the KGB. For many years it was known as Department Thirteen, until it became the completely independent Department V. In fact, Bond's Service had allowed all but its inner circle to go on referring to Department V for a long time after it had also disappeared from the secret Russian scene.

What had occurred was very much the business of the Secret Intelligence Service, which had been running an agent of its own—Oleg Lyalin—deep within Department V. When Lyalin defected, in the early seventies, it took little time for the KGB to discover he had been a long-term mole, and when that happened, Department V suffered a purge that virtually put it out of business.

Even Bond had not been informed, until relatively recently, that his old enemies were now completely reformed under the title Department Eight of Directorate S. So, he now thought, the most possible dark horses in the race for his head would be Department Eight of Directorate S, KGB.

In the meantime, though, there were very pressing problems. Check out the rooms that he thought contained the girls, and do something about getting out of the apartment block. The Bentley Mulsanne Turbo, beautiful and efficient car though it is, cannot be called the most discreet of vehicles. Bond reckoned that, with the alert still on, he could get about half a kilometer before being picked up.

Searching Der Haken's swinging body was not pleasant but it did yield the Bentley keys, if not those to the guest bedrooms or to the elevator. The telephone was still working, so at least there was communication with the outside world, though he had no way of making a clandestine call.

Carefully he dialed the direct number for the Service Resident in Vienna. It rang nine times before a fuddled voice responded.

"It's Predator," Bond spoke quickly, using his field cryptonym. "I have to speak clearly, even if the Pope himself has a wire on your phone."

"Right." The Resident was wide awake as soon as he recognized that it was Bond. "Where the hell are you? There's a great deal of trouble. A senior Austrian police officer—"

"And four of his friends got killed," Bond completed.

"They're out in droves looking for you . . . How did you know about the cop?"

"Because he didn't get killed."

"What?"

"Well, he did, but not in the accident. The bastard was doubling. Set it up himself," Bond went on to explain the situation in the simplest possible terms, telling the truth about everything that had occurred.

"Where are you?" The Resident's even voice carried undertones of concern.

123

"Somewhere in the new town, in a very plush apartment block, together with five corpses and, I hope, the two ladies who were with me. I haven't a clue about the address, but there's a telephone number you can work from." He read out the number on the handset.

"Enough to be going on with. I'll call you back as soon as I get something sorted, though I suspect they're going to ask you a lot of questions."

"The hell with the questions, just let me get out to the Klinik and on with the job. Quickly as you can." Bond took the initiative in closing the line. He then went to the first of the two locked rooms and banged on the door, hard. This time, he thought he could hear muffled exasperated grunts coming from inside.

The lock was Chubb—a deadlock again, like the one on the room he had been put into. It would have to be brute force, he thought, and to hell with the noise.

On his way to search for a suitable instrument in the kitchen, he went through the same procedure with the other locked room. The results were similar, and in the kitchen he found a heavy meat cleaver. The cleaver was sharp and, though he could never claim it went through the door like a warm knife through butter, it did the job on the first lock in around four minutes.

Sukie Tempesta lay on the bed, bound, gagged

and stripped to her underwear. "They took my clothes!" she shouted angrily when he got the ropes untied and the gag off.

"So I see," Bond smiled, and she reached for a blanket as he went quickly to the other room. The lock took less time—two minutes flat.

Nannie was in the same situation, and she yelled, "They stole my clothes, and my garter belt with the holster on it."

At that moment the telephone started to ring.

"A very senior officer's on the way with a team," the Resident said. "For heaven's sake be discreet, and tell only what truth is necessary. Then get to Vienna with all speed. That's an order from on high."

"Tell them to bring women's clothes," Bond snapped, giving a rough estimate of the sizes, but by the time he was off the telephone he could hear squeals of delight from the girls. They had found the clothes bundled in cupboards in one of the bathrooms.

Sukie came through, fully dressed; but, almost blatantly, Nannie appeared doing up her stockings to her retrieved garter belt, which still had holster and pistol in place.

"Let's get some air in here." Sukie went toward the windows and Bond had to put his body in front of her, saying that he would not advise opening even the curtains, let alone the windows. Quietly, he told both girls why, cautioned them to stay in the main room and then made his own way behind the drapes to let air into the room.

By the time he was back in the room the main doorbell was ringing violently.

Half the Salzburg police force appeared to have arrived, but they were headed by a smart, authoritative, gray-haired man whom they treated with great respect. He introduced himself as Kommissar Becker and allowed the investigative team to get on with their job on the terrace while he talked to Bond. The girls were taken away by plainclothes men—presumably to be interrogated separately in other rooms.

Becker came quickly to the point, and knew the score—"I have been instructed by our Foreign Ministry, and Security Department," he began. "I also understand that the Head of the Service to which you belong has been in touch. All I want from you is a detailed statement. You will then be free to go, but, Mr. Bond, I think it would be advisable for you to be out of Austria within twenty-four hours."

"Is that an order? Official?"

Becker shook his head. He had a long patrician nose and eyes in which a kindly streak moved when he allowed it. "No, not official. It is merely my personal opinion. Something I would advise. Now, Mr. Bond, let us take it from the top, as they say in musical circles."

Bond had a foolish image of Mozart, in front of a

small orchestra, saying, "From the top—a-one-two-three-four."

He recounted the whole story—leaving out all he knew about Tamil Rahani and SPECTRE's Head Hunt, so passing off the autobahn shoot-out as one of those occupational hazards that can unexpectedly befall any person in the kind of clandestine work in which he was involved.

"There is no need to be coy about your status." Becker gave him an avuncular smile. "In police work, here in Austria, we come into contact with all kinds of strange people, from many walks of American, British, French, German and Russian life—if you follow me. We are almost a clearinghouse for spies, only I know you don't like to use that word."

"It is a touch old-hat," Bond found himself smiling back. "In many ways we are outdated, old-fashioned people whom many would like to see consigned to the scrap heap. Electronics, satellites, computers and analysts have taken over much of our day-to-day operations."

"The same with us," the policeman shrugged. "However, nothing can replace the policeman on the beat, and I'd wager there is still a need for the man on the ground in your business. It applies to war also. However many tactical or strategic missiles appear over the horizon, the military needs live bodies in the field of action. Here we are geographically placed at a dangerous crossroads. We have a saying especially for the NATO powers—if the Russians come they will be with us, in Austria, for breakfast; but they will have their afternoon tea in London."

With a detective's knack of moving from a digressional tributary back to the mainstream of interrogation, Becker asked about the motives of Heinrich Osten—Der Haken—and Bond gave him a word-by-word account of what had passed between them, again leaving out the core of the business concerning the Head Hunt. "He has apparently been looking for a chance to line his pockets, and get away, for many years."

Becker gave a wry smile. "It doesn't surprise me. Der Haken, as most people called him, had an odd hold over the authorities. There are still many folk, some in high office, who recall the old days, the Nazis. They remember Osten all too well, I fear. Whoever brought him to this unpleasant end has done us a favor." Again, he switched his tack, "Tell me, why do you think the ransom has been set so high on these two ladies?"

James Bond tried his innocent expression. "I don't really know the terms of the ransom. In fact, I have yet to be told the full story of the kidnapping."

The distinguished police officer repeated his wry smile, this time wagging a finger as though Bond was a naughty schoolboy. "Oh, I believe you know the terms well enough. After all, you were in Osten's company for some time following the exaggerated reports of his death. I took over the case last night. The ransom is *you* Herr Bond, and you know it. Thee's also the little matter of ten million Swiss Francs lying, literally, on your head."

Bond made a capitulatory gesture. "Okay, so the hostages are being held against me, and your colleague found out about the contract, which is worth a lot of money. . ."

"Even if you *had* been responsible for his death," Becker cut in, "I don't think many police officers, either here or in Vienna, would go out of their way to charge you—Der Haken being what he was." He lifted an inquisitorial eyebrow.

"You didn't kill him, did you?"

"You've had the truth from me. No, I didn't, but I think I know who did."

Becker gave a sage nod. "Without even knowing the details of the kidnapping?"

"Yes. Miss May—my housekeeper—and Miss Moneypenny are bait. It's me they want. The two ladies are but a lure: tethered goats. These people know I will not hesitate to try to rescue the ladies and, I suspect, they're also certain I'd give myself up to save them."

"I thought English gentlemen only saved damsels in distress—fair maidens, young and innocent, held against their will by dragons. You are prepared to give your life for an elderly spinster and a colleague of uncertain age. . . ?"

"Also a spinster," Bond smiled. "The answer to

your question is yes. Yes, I would do that—though I intend to do it without losing my head."

"From my information about you, Herr Bond, you have many times almost lost your head over . . ."

"What we used to call a bit of fluff?" Bond smiled again.

"That is an expression I do not know—bit of fluff."

"Bit of fluff; piece of skirt—young woman," he supplied.

"Yes. Yes, I see, and you are correct. Our records show you as a veritable Saint George slaying dragons to save young, attractive women. This is an unusual situation for you. I—"

Bond cut in, sharply. "Sir, can you tell me what actually happened? How the kidnapping took place?"

Kommissar Becker paused as a plainclothes officer came into the room and there was a quick exchange, the officer telling his superior that the women had been interrogated. Becker dismissed him, saying they should all wait for a short time. Out on the balcony the scene-of-the-crime team was finishing up its preliminary investigation.

"Inspector Osten's case notes are, naturally, a shade hazy," the Kommissar finally said. "But we do have some bare details—his interviews with the Director of the Klinik, Herr Doktor Kirchtum, and others."

"Well?"

"Well, it appears that your colleague, Miss Moneypenny, visited the patient twice. After the second occasion she telephoned the Herr Direktor asking permission to take Miss May out—to a concert. It was all very innocent, and untaxing. The doctor gave his consent. Miss Moneypenny arrived, as arranged, in a car with a chauffeur and another man."

"There is a description?"

"The car was a BMW . . ."

"The man?"

"A silver BMW. A Series 7. The chauffeur was in uniform, and the man went into the Klinik with Miss Moneypenny. The staff who saw them said he was young, in his mid-thirties—light hair, neat, well-dressed, tall and muscular."

"And Moneypenny's behavior?"

"A little edgy, but nothig to speak of. Just a shade nervous. Miss May was in good spirits. One nurse noticed that Miss Moneypenny treated her with great care. The nurse said it was as though your Miss Moneypenny had nursing experience; she also said she had the impression that the tall, fair young man knew something about medicine. He stayed very close to Miss May the whole time." He sucked in breath through his teeth. "They got into the BMW and drove off. Four hours later, Herr Doktor Kirchtum received a telephone call saying they had been abducted. You know the rest."

"I do?" Bond queried.

"You were told. You started out toward Salzburg—then the shoot-out and your experience with the late unmourned Heinrich Osten."

"The car? The BMW?"

"Has not been sighted, which means that it was out of Austria very quickly, with plates changed—maybe a respray—or it's tucked away somewhere until all goes quiet."

"And there's nothing else?"

It was as though the Kommissar remained uncertain whether to pass on any further information. He did not look at Bond, but away, toward the scene-of-the-crime people taking their photographs and measurements on the terrace. Then, "Yes. Yes, there is one other thing. It was not in Osten's investigation notes, but they had it on the general file at headquarters." He hesitated again, and Bond had to prompt him.

"What was on file?"

"At 15:10, on the afternoon of the kidnapping—that is, around three hours before it took place—Austrian Airlines received an emergency booking from the Klinik Mozart. The caller said they had two very sick ladies who had to be transported to Frankfurt. There is a flight at 19:05—OS 421—arrives Frankfurt (Main) at 20:15. On that particular evening there were few passengers. The booking was made and accepted."

"And the ladies made the flight?"

132

"They were accommodated in first class. On stretchers. Both ladies were unconscious, and their faces covered with bandages . . ."

Classic KGB ploy, Bond thought. They had been doing it for years. He particularly recalled the famous Turkish incident, and there had been two at Heathrow, London.

"They were accompanied," Kommissar Becker continued, "by two nurses and a doctor. The doctor was a young, tall, good-looking man with fair hair."

Bond nodded, "And further inquiries showed that no such reservation had been made from the Klinik Mozart."

"Exactly," the Kommissar raised his eyebrows. "One of our men followed up the booking—sort of freelance, certainly Inspector Osten did not instruct him to do it."

"And?"

"And they were met by a genuine ambulance team at Frankfurt. They transferred onto another flight—the Air France 749, arriving Paris 21:30. It left Frankfurt on schedule, at 20:25. The ambulance people just had time to complete the transfer. We know nothing about what happened at the Paris end, but the kidnap call was placed to Doctor Kirchtum at 21:45. So, they admitted the abduction as soon as the victims were safely away."

"Paris?" Bond queried, absently. "Why Paris?"

and, as though in answer to his thoughts, the telephone began to ring. Becker himself picked it up and said nothing, just waiting for an identification on the line. His eyes flicked toward Bond, alarm stirring deeply within them. "For you," he mouthed quietly, hand over the mouthpiece.

He took the handset and identified himself. There was a moment's pause, after which Bond heard the voice of the Herr Doktor Kirchtum. His voice still had its resonance, but the Herr Doktor was obviously a very frightened man, for there was a definite tremor in his tone, and a number of pauses, as though he was being prompted. "Herr Bond," he began, "Herr Bond, I have a gun . . . They have a gun . . . It is in my left ear, and they say they will pull the trigger if I don't give you the correct message."

"Go on," Bond said calmly.

"They know you are with the police. They know you have been ordered to go to Vienna. That is what I must first tell you."

So, Bond thought, they had a wire on this telephone and had listened to his call to the Resident in Vienna.

Kirchtum continued, very shaky indeed. "You are not to tell the police of your movements."

"No. Okay. What am I to do?"

"They say they have booked a room for you at the Goldener Hirsch . . ."

134

"That's impossible. You have to book months ahead . . ."

The quaver in Kirchtum's voice became more pronounced. "I assure you, Herr Bond, for these people, nothing is impossible. They understand you have two ladies with you. They say they have a room reserved for them also. It is not the fault of the ladies that they have been . . . have been . . . I'm sorry, I cannot read the writing . . . Ah, have been implicated. For the time being these ladies will stay at the Goldener Hirsch, you understand?"

"I understand."

"You will stay there and await instructions. You will tell the police to keep away from you. You will on no account contact your people in London, not even through your man in Vienna. I am to ask if this is understood."

"It is understood."

"They say, good, because if it is not understood, the ladies—Miss May and her friend—will depart, and not peacefully."

"IT IS UNDERSTOOD!" Bond shouted at the mouthpiece.

There was a moment's silence. "The gentlemen here wish to play a tape for you. Are you ready?"

"Go ahead."

There was a click at the other end of the line, then May's voice, unsteady, but still the same old May,

135

"Mr. James, some foreign friends of yorn seem to hae the idea that I can be afeard easy. Dinna worry aboot me, Mr. Jam—" There was a sudden slap as a hand went over her mouth, then Moneypenny's voice, thick with fear, sounded as though she was standing behind him. "James!" she cried, "Oh, God, James . . . James . . ." and then an unearthly scream cut into his ear, loud, terrified, gibbering, and obviously coming not from Moneypenny, but from May.

It was the kind of prolonged, agonized shriek of horror that one associated with nightmares, ghosts and more especially, medieval devils. Coming from May, it made Bond's blood run cold. It was enough to put him under new orders—the orders and discipline of those who had May and Moneypenny in their power, for it would take something particularly terrifying to make the tough May scream like this. Bond was, at that moment, ready to obey them to the death.

He looked up. Becker was staring at him. Deep in the policeman's eyes there lurked a shocked expression. "For pity's sake, Kommissar, you didn't hear any of that conversation."

"What conversation?" Becker's expression did not alter.

— 9 —

Vampire

SALZBURG WAS CROWDED—a large number of United States citizens were out to see Europe before they died, and an equally large number of Europeans were out to see Europe before it completely changed into Main Street Common Market, with the same plastic frozen food everywhere and identical dull souvenirs from Taiwan on sale in all the major historic cities. Many thought they were already too late, but Salzburg, with the ghost of Mozart, and its own particular charm, did better than most.

The hotel Goldener Hirsch—the "Golden Hind," if one fancied loose translations—held up exceptionally well, especially as its charm, comfort and hospitality reached a long arm back through eight hundred years.

They had to use one of the Festival Hall car parks

and send over for the luggage—with the exception of Bond's two special briefcases—as the Goldener Hirsch stood right in the old town, where no car had ever gone before—between the Festival Hall and the crowded, colorful Getreidegasse, with its exquisite carved window frames, and the gilded wrought iron hanging shop signs, which gave it a clean air of distinction.

Sukie and Nannie were slightly bemused at the abrupt end to the night's dramas, both talking at once, trying to discover the whys and wherefores of the past twenty-four hours.

Bond calmly told them that the problem was his; that he would try to make it up to them somehow at a later date, and that they would almost certainly only have to bear with him for another twenty-four hours or so. "There are bookings for us at the Goldener Hirsch."

"Whaaat?" From Sukie.

"How in the name of Blessed Saint Michael did anyone get reservations?" From Nannie.

"Influence," Bond countered soberly. Then, after a short pause, "Why Saint Michael?"

"Michael the Archangel. Patron saint of bodyguards and minders."

Bond thought grimly that he needed all the help the angels could provide. Heaven alone knew what instructions would come to him within the next twenty-four hours at the Goldener Hirsch—or

138

whether the instructions would be in the form of a bullet or knife.

Before they left the Bentley, Nannie cleared her throat and began a lecture. "James," she began primly, "you just said something that Sukie finds offensive, and that doesn't make me happy either."

"Oh?"

"You said we'd only have to bear with you for another twenty-four hours or so."

"Well, it's true."

"No! No, it isn't true."

"I was accidentally forced to involve you both in a potentially very dangerous situation. I had no option but to drag you into it. You've both been courageous, and a great help, but it couldn't have been fun. What I'm telling you now is that you'll both be out of it within twenty-four hours or so."

"We don't want to be out of it," Nannie said calmly.

"Yes, it's been hairy," Sukie began, "but we feel that we're your friends. You're in trouble, and—"

"Sukie's instructed me to remain with you. To mind you, James, and, while I'm at it, she's coming along for the ride."

"That just might not be possible." Bond looked at each girl in turn, his clear blue eyes hard and commanding.

"Well, it'll just have to become possible," Sukie was equally determined.

"Look, Sukie, it's quite probable that I shall be given instructions from a very persuasive authority. They may well demand that you be left behind, released, ordered to go your own sweet way."

"Well," Nannie was just as firm, "it's just too bad if our own sweet way happens to be the same as your own sweet way, James. That's all there is to it."

Bond shrugged. It was possible that he would be ordered to take the women with him anyway. If not, there should be opportunity to leave quietly when the time came. The third possibility was that it would all end here, at The Goldener Hirsch, in which case the question would not arise.

"I might need some stamps," Bond said, quietly, to Sukie as they approached the hotel. "Quite a lot. Enough for a small package to the UK. Could you get them? Send a few innocuous postcards via the porter, and gather some postage stamps for me, would you."

"Penny stamp and a Chinese burn," muttered Nannie.

"I beg your pardon?" He looked at her curiously.

"It's the bully in her," Sukie said with a grin. "Schooldays. Penny stamp—on the foot—and a Chinese burn—twisting the wrist. Or didn't you do things like that at school, James?"

"Where did you two go to school, anyway?" he asked, giving them a suspicious look.

Sukie hung her head, "Sorry, James, *not* a convent. That's a fiction I find useful."

140

"A coeducational, so-called 'progressive' school in Surrey, actually." Nannie's face was set in innocence as she mentioned the name of a very expensive school, which, a few years ago, had been notorious. "Back in the bad old days when it got into the tabloids, and the local law turned it over for drugs every other week."

"Happiest days of your life." Sukie's grin had not left her face. "Oh, it's very respectable now, but when we were there—Oh my, oh my. There was one boy who had a secret still in the woods . . ."

"And we had an arsonist."

"They've cleaned it up now," Sukie sounded a shade sad. "*We're* not invited to open day because we were there during the dark age. Might corrupt the present flock, I suppose."

"Will you get me stamps?" Bond hissed.

"Of course, James." Sukie playfully trod on his foot. They reached the hotel entrance.

The Goldener Hirsch is perhaps the best hotel in Salzburg—enchanting, elegant and picturesque, though entering it is rather like walking onto the stage set of a superior production of *The White Horse Inn,* for the staff dressed in the local loden and the atmosphere was heavy with Austrian history. This in no way spoiled the charm, and the trio were met, by all, with a courtesy that successfully avoided the pseudo-fawning found in so many good European hotels.

Bond reflected that his room could easily have been especially prepared for shooting *The Sound of Music II,* but soon forgot that aspect as he set to work preparing for the possible dangers ahead.

He heard Kirchtum's warning again, clear in his head: "You will . . . *await instructions.* . . . You will on no account contact your people in London, not even through your man in Vienna." So, for the time being at least, it would be unwise to telephone London. Yet he *must* keep people informed.

From his second briefcase Bond extracted two minute tape recorders, checked battery strength, set them to voice activation, made certain the tapes were fully rewound and attached one—via a sucker microphone no larger than a grain of wheat—to the telephone; the other he placed in full view on top of the minibar, which looked more like an eighteenth-century commode than a minibar.

Fatigue had caught up with all of them, and he had arranged to meet the girls for dinner that evening in the famous snug bar around six. Until then, they had agreed to rest. He rang down for a pot of black coffee and a plate of scrambled eggs, and as he waited, Bond examined the rest of his room—and the small, windowless bathroom, with a neat shower, protected not by a curtain but by sliding, very solidly built glass doors. He approved, deciding to take a shower later. In the meantime, he unpacked, and was hanging suits in the wardrobe when the waiter arrived, in his fancy costume, with excellent coffee and

142

exceptionally well-prepared eggs.

The ASP was near at hand and, having put the *Do Not Disturb* sign, in four languages, on the door, Bond settled into one of the comfortable armchairs and began to doze.

The exhaustion had really caught up with him, for he eventually fell into a deep sleep, during which he dreamed, oddly, that he was a waiter in some continental café, the clientele of which included Sukie and Nannie. He seemed to spend the day dashing between the kitchen and the tables, waiting on M, Tamil Rahani, the now-deceased Poison Dwarf and the two girls.

Just before waking he had served Sukie and Nannie with tea and a huge cream cake, which turned to a lump of sawdust as soon as they tried to cut it. This appeared not to worry either of them, and they paid the bill, each one leaving a piece of jewelry as a tip. He reached to pick up a gold bracelet—left by Sukie—and it slipped, falling with a heavy crash onto a plate.

Bond woke with a start, convinced the noise was real. But now there only appeared to be the normal street noises drifting in through his window. He stretched, uncomfortable and stiff after sleeping in a chair, then glanced at the stainless steel Rolex on his wrist, amazed to see that he had slept for hours and that it was almost four-thirty in the afternoon.

He went, bleary-eyed, to the bathroom, feeling vaguely doped with sleep, turned on the lights and opened the tall doors to the shower. A strong hot shower, followed by one of icy temperature, would freshen him up. Then a shave and change of clothes. He just had good time to be ready for the girls at six o'clock.

It crossed his mind that whoever had made the present arrangements, and instructed him to await orders, was taking his time. He began to run the shower, closed the door and started to strip. If he had been manipulating this kidnapping and death hunt, Bond would have struck almost as soon as his victim had registered at the hotel, given orders for a move quickly and had his quarry out in the open while he was still groggy from a night without sleep. So far, there had been no contact, no directions. It was, of course, quite possible that his shadowy pursuers were preparing to, literally, take him out of the hotel itself.

Naked, he went back into the main room for the ASP and the baton, which he placed on the floor, under a couple of hand towels, just outside the shower. Then, after testing the water to check it was not too scalding for him to bear, Bond stepped under the spray, closed the sliding door and began to soap himself, rubbing his body vigorously with a rough flannel.

Thoroughly drenched with the hot spray, and rejoicing in a luxurious sense of cleanliness, he altered the settings on the taps, allowing the water to cool quickly, until he stood under a shower of almost ice-cold water. The shock hit him, like a man walking from the warmth of his home into a blizzard. Refreshed, he turned off the water, shaking himself like a dog, feeling a new, revitalized person. He rubbed his face with the flannel and reached out to open the sliding door.

As he did so, Bond became suddenly alert, his extra intuitive senses clicking on like a guidance system. In a fraction of a second he could almost smell danger nearby, and before his hand touched the door handle the lights went out, leaving him disoriented for a second, and in that second his hand missed the handle, though he heard the door slide open a fraction and close again with a thud.

This time, in the darkness, he knew he was not alone. There was something else in the shower with him, brushing his face, and then going wild, thudding against his body and the sides of the shower.

The thing's panic all but transferred itself to Bond, who scrabbled for the door with one hand, whirling the flannel about his face and body to ward off the unseen evil that flapped and bounced around the confined space of the shower, but when his fingers closed over the handle and pulled, the door would not move. The creature was becoming more violent, and, as he tugged hopelessly at the door, so its attacks seemed to become more vicious—he felt something claw at his shoulder, then at his neck, but managed to dislodge it, still hauling on the door, which refused to budge, jammed tight from outside.

The attacks ceased for a moment, as though what-

ever it was had paused to align itself for a final assault.

He waited, still tugging at the door, the flannel
held in front of him, whirling in the darkness. Then
Sukie's voice from far away, bright, even flirtatious,
"James? James, where the hell are you?"

"Here! Bathroom! Get me out, for heaven's sake!"
A second later, the lights went on again. He was
aware of Sukie's shadow in the main bathroom, but
he could now see his adversary. It was something he
had only come across in zoos before this, and even
then never one as big. Hunched on top of the spray
attachment sat a giant vampire bat, its evil eyes bright
above the razor-toothed mouth as it crouched, wings
spreading as it prepared to launch another attack.

He lunged at it with the sopping flannel, shouting
as he did so, "Get the shower open!"

A second later, the door began to slide. "Get out
of the bathroom, Sukie. Get out!" and he pulled back
the door as the creature moved.

Bond fell, sideways, into the bathroom, slamming
the shower door closed as he did so and rolling across
the floor, one hand going for the weapons under the
towels.

By itself a vampire bat could not kill instantly, he
knew that, and it gave him confidence, but the
thought of what it could inject into his bloodstream
was enough to make Bond feel true terror in the pit
of his stomach; and he had not been quick enough,

146

VAMPIRE

for the beast had also escaped into the main
bathroom.

He shouted again for Sukie to close the door and
wait. In a matter of two heartbeats all he knew of the
Desmodus rotundus—even its Latin name—flashed
through his head. There were three varieties; they
usually hunted, quietly, at night, creeping up on their
prey, clamping onto a hairless part of the body with
the incredibly sharp canine teeth, sucking blood and
pumping out saliva to stop the blood clotting. It was
the saliva that could transmit disease—anything from
rabies to forms of deadly virus.

This particular bat—now out of its element of
darkness—was obviously a hybrid, which probably
meant it carried something particularly horrible in its
saliva. The lights of the bathroom had completely
disoriented it, though it obviously needed blood badly
and would fight to sink its teeth into Bond's flesh.
The body, he saw now, was about 27 cm long, while
the wingspan spread a good 60 cm—over three times
the length of a normal member of its species.

It was certainly not possible to train a creature like
this, but if you could develop a hybrid of the
Desmodontidae family, it would be quite feasible to do it
along aggressive, belligerent lines.

As though sensing Bond's quick thoughts, the
huge bat raised its front legs, opening the wings to
full span and gathering its body up for the fast attack.

Bond's right hand flicked downward, clicking the

baton into its open position and smashing the weapon hard in the direction of the oncoming creature. It was luck more than fast judgement, for bats, with their strange radarlike senses, can, more often than not, avoid objects. Probably the unnatural light had something to do with it, but the steel baton caught it directly on the head, throwing it across the room to strike against the shower doors.

Bond could not let it rest there. With a stride he was over the twitching, flapping body, and like a man demented with fear, he hit the vile squirming animal again and again. He knew what he was doing, and was aware that fear played no small part in it, but as he struck the shattered body time after time his thoughts were of the man, or men, who had prepared such a thing as this, warping and redeveloping nature especially to kill him—for he had little doubt that the saliva of this particular vampire bat contained something that would bring a painful death much more quickly than rabies.

When he had finished, he dropped the baton into the shower, turned on the spray and walked toward the door. He had some disinfectant in the small, comprehensive first-aid kit that Q Branch provided.

He had forgotten about his nakedness.

"Well, now I've seen everything. Quits," said Sukie, unsmiling, from the chair in which she waited. There was a small pistol, similar to the one Nannie carried, in her right hand. It pointed steadily midway between Bond's legs.

— 10 —

The Mozart Man

Sukie looked hard at Bond, and then down at the gun. "It's a pretty little thing, isn't it?" She smiled, and he thought he could detect relief in her eyes.

"Just stop pointing it at me, put on the safety catch and then stow it away, Sukie."

She broadened the smile—and he could now see distinct relief flood her face. "Same goes for you, James."

Suddenly, Bond was aware of his nakedness, and grabbed at a hotel toweling robe, thrown over a chair, as Sukie, showing a remarkable slash of thigh, fitted the small pistol into a holster attached to her white garter belt. "Nannie fixed me up with this. Just like hers." She looked up at him, primly pulling down her skirt. "I brought your stamps, James. What was going on in there?" A nod toward the bathroom. "For a horrible moment I thought you were having real trouble."

"I *was* having trouble, Sukie. Very unpleasant trouble in the shape of a large hybrid vampire bat, which is not an animal one usually comes across anywhere in Europe, let alone in Salzburg. This one was definitely prepared by somebody."

"A vamPIRE BAT?" Her voice rose to a screech. "James! Jee-rusalem! Something like that could have . . ."

"Probably killed me. If some expert has been clever enough to breed a thing that size, they've almost certainly made sure it's carrying something more quickly lethal than rabies or bubonic plague. How did you get in, by the way?"

"I brought your stamps, as I said." She laid the little colored gummed strips on the table. "I knocked. No reply. Then realized the door was open. It wasn't until I heard the noises coming from the bathroom that I switched the light on. Someone had jammed the shower door with a chair. To be honest with you, I thought it was a practical joke—it's the kind of thing Nannie gets up to—until I heard you shout. I kicked the chair out of the way and ran like a deer."

"And waited in here with a loaded gun."

"Well, Nannie's teaching me to use it. She seems to think it's necessary."

"And I think it's really necessary for the two of

you to disappear, but thinking won't make it happen, if women have set their minds on something. Like to do me another favor?"

"Whatever you want, James." Her attitude was suspiciously soft, even yielding. Bond wondered if a girl like Sukie Tempesta could have the guts to handle a box containing a very dangerous hybrid vampire bat and let it loose in his shower. Someone had, and he would put money on the Principessa Tempesta being quite capable of such an act.

"I want you to get me some rubber gloves and a large bottle of antiseptic."

"Done." She stood up. "Any particular brand?"

"Something very strong." The small bottle of stuff in his first-aid kit would not be enough, he had realized, and nobody but an idiot would touch the bat's corpse without taking every possible precaution.

She left without either word or question, and Bond—now dry under the robe—got the small bottle of antiseptic from the first-aid kit and rubbed it hard over every inch of his flesh. By the time he finished, he smelled like a hospital casualty ward, so Bond tried to counteract the strong antiseptic smell with cologne. Only then did he start to dress.

There were considerable worries about disposing of the bat's body. Really it should be incinerated, and the bathroom needed a specialist's attention. Heaven knew what loathsome germs were carried by the creature. Bond knew he could not very well go to the

151

hotel manager and explain the circumstances. Antiseptic, a couple of hotel plastic carriers, a quick visit to the kitchens and their waste-disposal unit, then hope for the best, he thought.

In honor of an evening with the two girls, and in spite of the cloud of danger hanging over all of them, he put on his grey Cardin suit, a light blue shirt by Hilditch & Key of Jermyn Street and a navy white-spotted tie—Cardin again. He was just setting the tie when the telephone rang. As Bond picked it up he glanced at the tape hookup and saw the tiny cassette begin to turn as he answered with a curt "Yes."

It was Herr Doktor Kirchtum again. He sounded, if possible, even more frightened than before. "Mr. Bond?" a heavy, uneven breath. "Is that you, Mr. Bond?"

"Yes, Herr Direktor, are you all right?"

"Physically, yes. They say I am to speak the truth and tell you what a fool I've been."

"Oh?"

"Yes, I tried to refuse to pass any further instructions to you. I told them they should do this job themselves."

"And they did not take too kindly to that." Bond paused, then added, "Particularly as you had already told me I must come, with the two ladies, to the Goldener Hirsch, here in Salzburg." This last was for the sake of the tape.

"They took most unkindly," he sounded on the verge of tears, and the tremor in his voice became

152

more apparent. "I must now give you instructions quickly, they say, otherwise they will use the electricity again."

"Go ahead. Fast as you like, Herr Doktor." He knew what Kirchtum was talking about—the brutal, old, but effective method of attaching electrodes to the genitals. Outdated methods of persuasion were often quicker than the drugs used among more sophisticated interrogators nowadays.

Kirchtum's voice became rapid and high with fear, so that Bond could almost see a pair of hoods—from one organization or another—standing over him, hands poised on the switch. "You are to go to Paris. Tomorrow. It should only take you one day. You must drive on the direct route, and there are rooms booked for you at the George V."

"You mean the ladies have to accompany me?"

"This is essential . . . you understand? Please say you understand, Mr. Bond."

"I—" He was interrupted by a hysterical, terrible scream. The hood had obviously pulled the switch just for encouragement.

"I understand."

"Good." It was not the Herr Doktor's voice now, but a hollow, distorted sound, as though the speaker was using some voice distortion electronics. "Good. Then you will save the two ladies that we hold from a most unpleasant and slow end to their earthly travails. Do it, Bond. We shall speak in Paris."

The line closed, and Bond picked up the miniature tape machine, running the tape back and replaying it through its tiny speaker. At least he could now get this to either Vienna or London so that they would know the course of his movements. Also, the final echoing voice on the line might be some small help to them. Even if the hoods who were terrorizing Kirchtum had used an electronic "voice handkerchief," there was still the chance that Q Branch might take an accurate voice print from it. At least, if they could make some identification, M would know which particular organization Bond was dealing with.

He went over to the desk, removed the microcassette from the tape machine, nipping off the little plastic safety lug in order to prevent the tape from being accidentaly recorded over. He then took out the usual leather folder containing stationery, wrote a few words on a sheet of hotel notepaper and chose the stoutest envelope from the selection in the folder.

He addressed it to M's cover name as chairman of Transworld at one of the safe post office box numbers, folded the cassette into the paper and sealed the envelope.

Consulting the postage guide in the folder, he then selected a rough estimation of the correct stamps—he could only guess the weight of the package.

He had just finished this important chore when a knock at the door heralded Sukie's return. She carried a brown paper sack containing her purchases, and appeared inclined to stay in the room until Bond firmly suggested that she join Nannie and wait in the snug bar for him.

The job of cleaning up the bathroom, wearing the rubber gloves and using almost the entire bottle of antiseptic, took fifteen minutes and left him with a cleansed security baton and the ASP, together with a neat, sinister parcel containing the remains of the disgusting live weapon that had been used against him. Before completing the job he added the gloves to the parcel, and was 99 percent confident that no germs could have entered his system.

While he worked, Bond thought of the possibilities regarding the perpetrator of this last attempt on his life. He was almost logically certain that it was his old enemy, SMERSH—now Directorate S's Department Eight of the KGB—that was holding Kirchtum and using him as their personal messenger. But was it really their style to use such a thing as a hybrid vampire bat against him?

Who, he wondered now, would have the resources to work on the breeding and development of a weapon as horrible as this large vampire bat? It struck him that it must have taken a number of years to bring the creature to its present state, and that indicated a large organization, with funds and the specialist expertise required. The work would have been carried out in, at least, a simulated warm forestlike environment, for if his memory was correct, the original of the species could be found only in the jungles and forests of Mexico, Chile, Argentina and Uruguay.

Money, special facilities, time and zoologists without scruples. SPECTRE was the obvious bet, though any well-funded outfit with an interest in terrorism and killings would be on the list, for the creature would not have been developed simply as a one-off to inject some terrible terminal disease into Bond's bloodstream. The Bulgarians and Czechs favored that kind of thing, and he would not even put it past Cuba to send some agent of their well-trained internal G-2 out into the wider field of international skulduggery. The Honored Society (a polite term for the Mafia) was also a possibility—for they were not beyond selling the goods to terrorist organizations, as long as they were not used within the borders of the United States, Sicily or Italy.

When the chips were down, Bond plumped for SPECTRE itself—but once more during the strange choreography of this dance of death, someone had saved him, at the last moment, from another attempted execution, and this time it was Sukie, a young woman, met, seemingly, by accident. Could she, possibly, be the truly dangerous ace in the hole?

He sought out the kitchens and put on a great deal of charm, giving them a story about food left accidentally and embarrassingly in his car. There was an incinerator, and an odd-job man was summoned to lead him there to dispose of the bundle. The man even offered to do the thing himself, but Bond tipped him heavily, saying he would like to see it burned.

It was now six-twenty, but in spite of being late for his meeting with the girls, he made a last visit to his room to douse himself in cologne lest any traces of the antiseptic remained.

The girls were solicitous and anxious to hear his story, but Bond merely said they would be told all in good time. For the moment they must be content with the more pleasant things of life. They had a drink together in the famous snug bar, and then a splendid dinner—Nannie had been sensible enough to reserve a table—of that famous Viennese boiled beef dish they called Tafelspitz, which is like no other boiled beef on earth and is a gastronomic delight with its piquant vegetable sauce, served with sauteed potatoes that even Bond, not really a potato man, failed to resist.

They had no first course, as it is sacrilege not to eat dessert in an Austrian restaurant. They chose the obvious light, fragile queen of puddings, the Salzburg Souffle, said to have been created nearly three hundred years ago by a chef in the Hohensalzburg. It arrived, to the girls' consternation, topped by what looked like the north face of the Eiger in *Schlag*—as the locals call their rich whipped cream.

Thus replete, Bond led the girls outside into the warm air and among the strolling window-shoppers in the *Getreidegasse.* He wanted to be far away from any possible eavesdropping equipment for what he had to say.

"I'm bloated." Nannie appeared to be hobbling, one hand to her stomach.

"You're going to need the food with what the night has in store for us," Bond spoke quietly. "After today, dinner was not a time for nouvelle cuisine, I promise you."

"Promises, promises," Sukie muttered, breathing heavily. "I feel like a dirigible. So what's in store, James?"

He told them about the orders to drive to Paris. "You've made it plain that you're coming with me, whatever. The people giving me the run-around have also been clear in their demands. You *are* to accompany me, and I have to be sure that you do. The lives of a very dear friend and an equally dear colleague are genuinely at risk. I can say no more."

"Of course we're coming," Sukie bridled.

"Try and stop us," from Nannie, still bent almost double by the intake of food.

"I'm going to do one thing out of line," he explained. "The orders are that we make the drive tomorrow—which I presume means they expect us to do it in daylight. I'm starting just after midnight. That way I can plead that we did start the drive tomorrow, but we might just be a jump ahead of them.

It's not much, but I'll do anything to throw them, even slightly, off balance."

The girls agreed to meet him by the car on the dot of midnight, and after a few more words, they started to retrace their steps toward the Goldener Hirsch.

On the return journey, Bond paused, for a brief moment, turned quickly toward a mailbox set into the wall, and slid his package from breast pocket to the box. It was neatly done, taking a minimum of time, and only very close surveillance would have spotted it. He was fairly certain that the action was not noticed even by the girls.

It was just after ten when he got back to his room, and by ten-thirty the briefcases and his bag were packed, and he had changed into casual jeans and jacket—the ASP and baton nestling in their appropri-ate hiding places. With an hour and a half to go be-fore his meeting with the girls, James Bond sat down and concentrated on how he could possibly gain the initiative in this wild and dangerous death hunt.

So far, the attempts on his life had been cunning, or only in their early stages, when someone else had stepped in to save his hide and, he presumed, set him up for the final act in the drama. Rule one was to trust nobody—especially Sukie, now that she had revealed herself as his savior, however unwitting, in the vam-pire bat incident. Next came the question of how to take some command. There appeared to be no possibility until he thought of the Klinik Mozart and its Herr Direktor, being held there. The last thing whoever was in control at the Klinik would expect was an assault on this power base.

It was a fifteen-minute drive out of Salzburg to the Klinik Mozart and time ran short. If he could find the right car, perhaps it was just possible.

Moving rapidly, Bond left the room and hurried downstairs to reception to ask what self-drive hire cars were available quickly. For once, Bond seemed to be making his own luck. There was a Saab 900 Turbo—a car to which he was well used—which had only just been returned. A few rapid telephone calls and it was waiting for him, only four minutes' walk from the hotel.

As he waited for the cashier to take details of his credit card, he walked the few paces to the interhouse telephones and rang Nannie's number. She answered straight away. "Say nothing," he spoke quietly. "Wait in your room. I may have to delay departure for an hour. Tell Sukie."

She muttered a surprised affirmative, and by the time he got back to the desk, all formalities had been completed.

Five minutes later, having collected the car from a smiling representative, Bond was driving skillfully out of Salzburg, taking the mountain road south, passing the strange Anif water tower, which rose, like an English manor house, from the middle of a pond in the Salzburg suburbs, then on, up almost as far as the town of Hallein, which originated as an island bastion in the middle of the Salzach and had its own musician to remember—Franz-xavier Gruber, composer of "Stille Nacht, Heilige Nacht," the carol known in all languages to all Christian people.

The Klinik Mozart stood back from the road, about a mile on the Salzburg side of Hallein, surrounded by woodland that screened the converted seventeenth-century house from passing view.

Bond pulled the Saab into a layby, switched off the headlights, cut the engine, put on the reverse lock and climbed out. A few moments later he had ducked under the wooden fencing and was moving carefully through the trees, peering into the darkness for his first glimpse of the Klinik—which he had seen only once before, when visiting to make arrangements for May. Now, he had no idea how those who held the Klinik had arranged for its defense; nor did he know how many people were there, using it as a tactical headquarters from which to maneuver Bond into the final net.

He reached the edge of the trees just as the moon came out. There were no exterior lights burning, so all he could see was the classic oblong block of the big house with light streaming from many of the twenty or thirty windows that fronted the building.

As his eyes adjusted, Bond tried to pick up movement across the hundred yards or so that separated him from the house. There were four cars parked on the wide gravel frontage, but no sign of life, except for the lighted windows. Gently he eased out the ASP, gripping it in his right hand, while his left removed the baton, which he flicked open, ready for instant use. Then he broke cover, moving fast and silently, remaining on the grass and avoiding the long drive that ended in the gravel parking area.

Nothing moved or cried out. He reached the gravel and tried to recall where the Herr Direktor's office lay in relation to the front door. Somewhere to the right, he thought, remembering how he had stood at the tall windows on his last visit, looking out at the lawns and drive. Now he had a fix, and more, for he recalled they were French windows—the French windows immediately to his right, brightly lit and with the curtains closed.

Moving sideways, he eased himself toward the windows, realizing, with heart thudding, that they were open and voices, muffled by the drapes, could be heard from inside. Now he was close enough to actually hear what was being said.

"You cannot keep me here forever—not with only three of you." It was the Herr Direktor whose voice he recognized first. The bluffness completely gone, replaced by a pleading note. "Surely you've done enough."

"We've managed so far." Someone else spoke. "You have been cooperative—to a point—Herr Direktor, but we cannot take chances. Only when the man Bond is secure, and with our people far away, can we leave. The situation is ideal for the short-wave transmitter and electronic surveillance on Bond; your patients have not suffered. Another twenty-four—maybe forty-eight—hours will make little difference to you. Eventually we shall leave you in peace."

"'Stille Nacht. Heilige Nacht,'" another voice chuckled, gruffly, and Bond's blood ran cold. He moved closer to the windows, the tips of his fingers resting against the inch-wide crack in their opening.

"You wouldn't. . . ?" There was real terror in Kirchtum's voice now—not hysterical fear, but the genuine, eighteen-carat terror that only strikes a man facing inevitable death by extreme torture.

"You've seen our faces, Herr Direktor. You know who we are."

"I would never . . ."

"Don't think about it. You have one more message to pass for us yet, when friend Bond gets to Paris. After that . . . well, we shall see."

Bond physically shivered at the voice, which he had already recognized and never thought, in a thousand years, to hear in this situation. He took a deep breath and slowly pulled, widening the crack between the windows, then inserting his fingers between the curtains to peer into the room.

Kirchtum was strapped into an old-fashioned desk chair—a round-bottomed affair made of wood

163

and leather, with three legs on castors, the kind of chair one saw in newspaper editors' offices in old movies, shown late on television. The bookcase behind him had been swept clean of books, which had been replaced by a powerful radio transmitter. One broad-shouldered man sat in front of the radio; another stood behind Kirchtum's chair, and their leader, legs apart, faced the Herr Direktor. Bond recognized him at once, just as he had known his voice, yet he could not believe it was he.

He breathed in through his nose, lifted the ASP and lunged through the windows. There was no time for sentiment, and what he had heard told him that the three men constituted the entire enemy force at the Klinik Mozart.

The ASP thumped four times, two bullets shattering the chest of the man behind Kirchtum's chair, the other two wrecking the back of the hood who sat before the radio.

The third man whirled around, mouth open, hand moving to his hip.

"Hold it there, Quinn! One move and your legs go—right?"

Steve Quinn, the Service's man in Rome, stood statue-still, his mouth curving into a snarl.

"Herr Bond? How. . . ?" Kirchtum's voice assumed a whisper.

"You're finished, James. No matter what you do to me, you're finished." Steve Quinn had not regained his composure, but he gave a reasonable impression of doing so.

"Not quite," Bond smiled, without triumph. "Not quite yet, though I admit being surprised to find you here, at the Mozart. Who're you really working for, Quinn? SPECTRE?"

Quinn gave him a fast grimace of a smile. "No. Pure KGB. Their mole. First Chief Directorate, naturally, for years, and not even Tabby knows. Now on temporary detachment to Department Eight, which at one time was your sparring partner, SMERSH. Also, unlike yourself, James, I've always been a Mozart man. I prefer to dance to good music."

"Oh, you'll dance." Bond's face showed the hard, cold and cruel streak that was the darkest side of his nature. "But it won't be to soft music."

— 11 —

Hawk's Wing and Macabre

JAMES BOND was not prepared to waste time. He knew, to his cost, the danger of keeping an enemy talking—it was a technique he had used to his own advantage, and Steve Quinn was quite capable of trying to play for time. Crisply, still keeping his distance, Bond ordered the man to stand a good five feet from the wall, spread his legs, stretch out his arms and then lean forward, palms against the wall. Once Quinn was in that position, Bond made him shuffle his feet back even further so that the man could not possibly use any leverage for a quick attack.

Only when he felt it was safe did Bond approach his captive, whom he frisked with great care. There was a small S & W Chief's Special revolver tucked into the waistband of his trousers, hard against the small of his back; a tiny automatic pistol—a Steyr 6.35mm Austrian weapon—taped to the inside of his left calf and a nasty little flick knife secured, with similar tape, to the outside of his right ankle.

"Haven't seen one of these in years." Bond tossed the Steyr onto the desk. "No grenades secreted up your backside, I trust." He did not smile. "You're a damned walking arsenal, man. You should be careful, terrorists might be tempted to break into you."

"In this game, I've always found it useful to be like a Boy Scout and be prepared." As he spoke the last word, Steve Quinn let his body sag. He collapsed onto the floor and, in the fraction of a second, flip-rolled to the right, his arm reaching toward the table where the Steyr automatic lay.

"Don't try it!" Bond snapped, bringing the ASP to bear.

Quinn was not ready either to meet his Maker or die for the cause to which he had allied himself—a traitor to the Service. He stopped, lying on the floor, the hand still raised, looking like a huge child playing the old game of statues.

"Face down! Spreadeagled!" Bond commanded, looking around the room for something to secure his prisoner. Keeping the ASP leveled at Quinn, he sidled behind Kirchtum, using his left hand to un- buckle the two short and two long straps, obviously made for restraining violent patients. As he moved he continued to snap orders at Quinn. "Face right down, eat the carpet, you bastard, and get your legs wider apart, arms in the crucifixion position."

He obeyed, grunting obscenities as he did so, and,

as the last buckle gave way, Kirchtum started to rub his wrists, arms, legs and ankles. The wrists were marked where the hard leather thongs had bitten into his flesh.

"Stay seated," Bond whispered. "Don't move. Give the circulation a chance." Taking the straps, he went toward Quinn, keeping his gun hand well back, knowing that a lashing foot could possibly catch his wrist. "The slightest move and I'll blow a hole in you so big that even the maggots'll need maps. Understand?"

Quinn grunted and Bond kicked his legs together, viciously planting the steel-capped toe of his shoe against the man's ankle so that he yelped with pain. While the agony was obviously sweeping through him, Bond swiftly slid one of the straps around the ankles, pulled hard and buckled the leather tightly.

"Now the arms! Fingers laced behind your back!" As though to make him understand, Bond gave the right wrist a jar with his foot. There was another cry of agony, but Quinn did as he was told, and another strap went around the wrists.

"This is old-fashioned, but it'll keep you quiet until we've made arrangements for something more permanent," Bond muttered as he buckled the pair of long straps together, fastening one end around Quinn's already secured ankles, then bringing the elongated strap up around his captive's neck and back to the ankles. He pulled tightly, bringing the prisoner's head up and forcing the legs toward his trunk. Indeed, it was a method old and well-tried. If the captive struggled all he did was strangle himself, for the straps were pulled so tightly that they made Quinn's body into a bow, the feet and neck being the outer edges. Even if he tried to relax his legs, the strap would pull hard on the neck.

Quinn let out a stream of obscene abuse, and Bond—very angry now at the thought of an old friend being revealed as a defector—kicked him hard in the ribs, took out a handkerchief and stuffed it into the trussed man's mouth with a curt, "Shut up!"

Now, for the first time since coming through the windows, he had a real chance to look around the room.

It was all very solid—heavy desk, the bookcases rising to the ceiling, the chairs with curved backs, circa 1850. Kirchtum still sat in the castored working chair, face pale, hands shaking—a big, expansive man turned to terrified blubber.

Bond went over to the bookcase that contained the radio, stepping over the books that lay in disorderly piles where they had fallen when the thugs had swept them from the shelves.

The radio operator remained slumped in his chair, blood still dripping onto the thick carpet, bright against its faded pattern. Bond pushed the body unceremoniously from the chair. He did not

169

recognize the face, twisted in the surprised agony of death. The other hood was sprawled against the wall, as if he were a drunk, collapsed at a party—except that drunks do not usually leave long trails of blood down the wall. This one was recognizable. Bond could not put a name to him, but had seen the photograph in the files—East German heavy, a criminal with terrorist leanings. It was amazing, he thought, how many of Europe's violent villains were turning into mercenaries for the terrorist cells. Rent-a-Thug, he thought, turning to Herr Doktor Kirchtum. "How did they manage it?" he asked—bland, as though all sensitivity had been drained from him by the discovery that Quinn had sold out.

"Manage. . . ?" Kirchtum appeared to be at a loss.

"Look . . ." Bond almost shouted, and then realized that he was facing a man whose English was not always perfect, and who was a gibbering wreck. He walked over and laid an arm on the man's shoulder, speaking quietly and comfortingly. "Look, Herr Doktor, I have to get information from you very quickly. Especially if we are to ever see the two ladies alive again."

"Oh, my God." Kirchtum covered his face with his banana bunch hands. "It is my fault that Miss May and her friend . . . Never should I have allowed Miss May to go out." He was near to tears.

"No. No, not your fault. How were you to know? Just tell me certain things. Be calm and answer my

170

questions as carefully as you can. First, how did these men manage to get in and hold you here?"

Kirchtum let his fingers slide down his face. The eyes were full of desolation. "Those . . . those two . . ." he gestured at the bodies, "they came as repair men for the *Antenne*—what you call it? The pole? For the television."

"The television aerial."

"Ja, yes, the television ayrial.   The duty sister let them in, and onto the roof. She thought it good, okay. Only when she was comink to me did I smell a mouse."

"They asked to see you?" He did not correct the doctor.

"In here. My office, they ask. Only later I find they had been putting up *Antenne* for their radio equipment. They lock the door. Threaten me with guns and torture. Tell me to put the next doctor in charge of the Klinik. To say I would be tied up, in my study on business matters for a day or two. They laughed when I had to say 'tied up.' They had pistols. Guns. What could I do?"

"You do *not* argue with loaded guns," Bond agreed, "as you can see," nodding to the pair of corpses. He turned his eyes to the grunting, straining Steve Quinn. "And when did this piece of scum crawl out of the gutter?"

"Later that night. Through the windows, like yourself."

171

"What night *was* this?"

"The day after the ladies disappeared. The two in the afternoon, the other at night. By then they had me in this chair. All the time, they had me here, except when I had to perform functions . . ."

Bond looked surprised, and Kirchtum said he meant natural functions. "In the end I refused to give you messages on the telephone. Until then they had only threatened me. But after that . . ."

Already Bond had seen the bowl of water and the electric socket containing a plug from which hung wires and a set of large crocodile clips. He nodded, knowing only too well what the Herr Doktor must have suffered. "And the radio?" he asked.

"Ah, yes. They used it quite often. Twice, three times a day."

"You hear any of it?" Bond looked at the radio. There were two sets of earphones jacked into the receiver.

"Most of it. They wear the earphones sometimes, but there are speakers there, see."

Indeed, there were two small circular speakers set into the center of the system. "Tell me about the messages."

"What to tell? They listen to you like magic. They spoke. Another man spoke from far away . . ."

"Who spoke first? Did the other man call them?"

Kirchtum appeared to be lost in thought for a

moment. Then, "Ah, yes. The voice would come with
a lot of crackling."

Bond, standing beside the sophisticated, high fre-
quency unit, saw that the dials were glowing. There
was a mild, almost distant hum from the speakers,
and he noted the dial settings. They were talking to
someone quite a long way off—it could be four hundred or four thousand miles, give or take a mile.

"Can you recall if the messages came at any spe-
cific times?"

Kirchtum's brow creased, and the large head nodded, "Yes. Ja. Yes, I think so. In the mornings. Early.
Six o'clock. Then at noon . . ."

"Six in the evening and again at midnight?"

"Something like that, yes. But not quite."

"Just before the hour, or just after, yes?"

"This is right."

"Anything else?"

The doctor paused, thought again, and then nodded. "Ja. I know they had to send a message when
news came that you had left. They have a man watching . . ."

"The hotel?"

"No. I heard the talk. He is watching the road.
He is to telephone when you drive away and they
were to make a signal with the radio. It is special
words . . ."

"Can you remember them?"

173

"Something about the package being posted to Paris."

That sounded par for the course, Bond thought. Cloak and dagger. The Russians, like the Nazis before them, read too many bad espionage novels. "Were there any other special words?"

"Ja, they used others. The man to the other end calls himself Hawk's Wing—I thought it strange."

"And here?"

"Here they call themselves Macabre."

"So, when the radio comes on, the other end says something like 'Macabre, this is Hawk's Wing . . .'"

"Over."

"Over, yes. And 'Come in Hawk's Wing.'"

"This is just how they say it, yes."

Suddenly, as though he had just thought of it, Bond asked about noise. "Why haven't any of your staff come to this office, or alerted the police? There must have been noise. I have used a gun."

Kirchtum shrugged. "The noise of your pistol might have been heard from the windows, but the windows only. My office is soundproofed. Sometimes there are disturbing noises from the Klinik. This is why the windows were open. They had them open only a few times a day for the circulation of air. It can get most heavy in here with the soundproofing. Even the windows are soundproofed with the double glaze."

Bond nodded and glanced at his watch. It was

now almost eleven-forty-five. Hawk's Wing would be making his call at any time, and he had already figured that Department Eight's watchdog would be stationed somewhere near the E-11 Autobahn. In fact they probably had all exit roads watched. Nice and professional. Far better than just one man at the hotel.

But he was now playing for time. Quinn had stopped twisting on the floor, and Bond was already beginning to work out a scheme that would take care of him. Quinn was an old professional, and even though he had defected, his experience and training would make him a hard man to influence. It would take days, even weeks, to crack him under ideal interrogation conditions; violence would be counterproductive. There was, he knew, only one possible way to get at Stephen Quinn.

He went over to the strapped figure, going down on one knee near his head. "Quinn," he said softly, and saw the hate in the man's eyes as they gave him a sidelong, painful and uncomfortable look. "We need your cooperation."

The man grunted through the makeshift gag. It was the kind of grunt which meant that in no way would Quinn cooperate.

"I realize the telephone is insecure, but I'm calling Vienna for a relay to London. I want you to listen very carefully." He went over to the desk, lifted the receiver and dialed 0222-43-16-08—the Tourist

175

Board offices in Vienna, where he knew there would be an answering machine at this time of night.

He held the receiver away from his ear so that Quinn would at least hear a muffled answer.

It came, and Bond simultaneously pressed the receiver very close to his ear and softly closed the line with his finger on the rest.

"Predator," he said, softly. Then, after a pause, "Yes. Priority for London to copy and action taken immediately—and I mean within minutes. Rome's gone off the rails." He paused again, as though listening. "Yes, working for Center. I have him, but we need extreme measures. I want a snatch team in Rome at Flat 28, 48 via Barberini—it's next to the JAL offices. Lift Tabitha Quinn and hold for orders, and tell them to alert Hereford to call one of the 'psychos' in if M doesn't want dirty hands."

Behind him, he heard Quinn grunting, trying to move, getting agitated. A threat against his wife was about the only thing that would keep the man in line.

"That's right. Will do. I'll run it through you, but termination or near termination might be necessary. I'll get back within an hour or so. Good." He put down the instrument, going to kneel beside Quinn again. This time the look in the man's eyes had changed, hatred was edged with anxiety.

"It's okay, Stephen Quinn. Nobody's going to hurt *you*. But I fear it could be different with Tabby. I'm sorry."

There was no way that Quinn could even suspect

176

a bluff or double bluff. He had been in the Service for a long time himself, and was well aware that calling in a "psycho," as the Service called its mercenary killers, was usually no idle threat. He knew it could happen. Worse, he was versed in the many ways his wife could suffer before death. Most of all, he had worked with Bond and was, therefore, sure 007 would show no compunction in carrying out the threat.

Bond went on talking. "I gather there will be a call coming through. I'm going to strap you into the chair in front of the radio. Make the responses fast. Get off the air quickly. Feign bad transmission if you have to. But, Steve, don't do anything out of line—no missing out words, or putting in 'alert' sentences. I'll be able to tell, as you know. Just as you'd be able to detect a dodgy response. If you *do* make a wrong move everything'll go black, and you'll wake up in Warminster to a long interrogation and a longer time in jail. You'll also be shown photographs of what they did to Tabby before she died. That I promise you. Now," he manhandled the man into the chair recently vacated by the dead radio operator, adjusting the straps from the strangulation position and rebinding him tightly into the chair.

He felt confident, for the fight appeared to have gone out of Steve Quinn. But you could never tell. The defector might well be so indoctrinated that he could bring himself to sacrifice his wife.

At last, he asked if Quinn was willing to play it

straight. The big man just nodded his head sullenly, and Bond pulled the gag from his mouth.

"You bastard!" Quinn said, sounding breathless and throaty.

"It can happen to the best of us, Steve. Just do as you're told and there'll be a chance that both of you will live."

Hardly had he completed the words when the radio hummed and crackled into life. Bond's hand went out to the receive-and-send switch, set to *Receive*.

Across the airwaves a disembodied voice recited the litany, "Hawk's Wing to Macabre. Hawk's Wing to Macabre. Come in Macabre."

Bond nodded to Quinn, clicked the switch to *Send*, and for the first time in years, prayed.

— 12 —
England Expects

"MACABRE, HAWK'S WING, I have you. Over."
Steve Quinn's voice sounded too steady for Bond's
liking, but there was no other option.

The voice at the distant end crackled through the
small speakers. "Hawk's Wing, Macabre, routine
check. Report situation. Over."

Quinn paused for a second, and Bond allowed the
muzzle of the ASP to touch him behind the ear. "Situation normal. We await developments. Over."

"Call back when package is on its way. Over."

"Wilco, Hawk's Wing. Over and out."

There was silence for a moment as the switch was
clicked to the *Receive* position again. Then Bond
turned to Kirchtum, asking if it all sounded normal.

"It was usual," he nodded.

"Right, Herr Doktor. Now you come into your

own. Can you get something that'll put this bastard to sleep for around four or five hours, and make him wake up feeling reasonable—no slurred speech or anything?"

"I have just the think." For the first time, Kirchtum smiled, easing his body painfully from the chair and hobbling off toward the door. Halfway there he realized that he was wearing no shoes or socks, so he limped back, retrieved the articles, put them on and slowly left the room.

"If you have by any chance alerted whoever that was on the line, you must remember that Tabby won't last long once we've found you out. You do everything by the book, Quinn, and I'll do my best for you as well. But the first person to be concerned about is your wife. Right?"

"Right." Quinn glared at him with the kind of hatred shown only by traitors who have been caught and cornered.

"This applies to honesty as well. I want straight answers, and I want them now."

"I might not know the answers."

"True, but if you do know them, you talk . . . otherwise—well, we'll know truth from fiction in the long run."

Quinn did not reply.

"First, what's going to happen in Paris? At the George V?"

180

"Our people're going to get you. At the hotel, at the George V."

"But you could've got me here. Heaven knows, enough people have already tried."

"Not my people. Not KGB. We banked on you coming down here after May and Moneypenny. Yes, *we* organized the kidnapping. The idea was to start manipulating you from here. Getting you to Salzburg was like putting you into a funnel."

"Then it wasn't your people who had a go in the car?"

"No. One of the competition. They took out the Service people. None of my doing. You seem to have had a guardian angel all the way. The two men I put on to you were from the Rome station. I was to burn them once they saw you safely into Salzburg."

"And send me on to Paris?"

"Yes. Blast you. If it was anyone else but Tabby, I'd . . ."

"But it *is* Tabby we're thinking about." Bond paused. There was a lot still to be done, and he had to know more. "Paris?" he asked again, "Why Paris?"

Quinn locked eyes with him. Deep in the eyes, Bond detected an indecision. The man *did* know something more. "Why Paris? Remember Tabby."

"It was either Berlin, Paris or London. They want your head, Bond. But they want to see it done. We were out to claim the reward, and to be away with the money once you'd been handed over. Just taking your head wasn't enough. My instructions were to get you to Paris. The people there have orders to pick you up, and—" He stopped, as though he'd already said enough.

"And deliver the package?"

Another fifteen seconds' silence. "Yes."

"Deliver it where?"

"To the Man."

"Tamil Rahani? The Head of SPECTRE?"

"Yes."

"Deliver it where?" Bond repeated.

No response.

"Remember Tabby, Quinn. I'll see Tabby suffer great pain before she dies. Then they'll come for you. Where am I to be delivered?"

The silence stretched for what seemed to be minutes. Then, "Florida."

"Where in Florida? Big place, Florida. Where? Disney World?"

Quinn looked away. "The southernmost tip of the United States," he said.

"Ah," Bond nodded. The Florida Keys, he thought. Those linked islands that stretched out one hundred miles into the ocean. Bahai Honda Key, Big Pine Key, Cudjoe Key, Boca Chica Key, the names of the most famous ones flicked through his head. Somewhere in there was Key Largo where, in a old movie, Bogart had bested Edward G. Robinson. But the southernmost tip—well, that was Key West, one-time home of Hemingway, a narcotics route, a tourist paradise, with a sprinkle of islands outside its reef. Ideal, thought Bond. Key West—who would have imagined SPECTRE setting up its headquarters there? "Key West," he said aloud, and Quinn gave a small, ashamed nod. "Paris, London or Berlin. Presumably they could have included Rome and other major cities. Anywhere they could get me onto a direct Miami flight, eh?"

"I suppose so."

"It's not a big place, but where, exactly, in Key West?"

"*That* I don't know. In all truth, I just do not know." He convinced Bond, who shrugged as though to say it did not matter.

The door opened and Herr Doktor Kirchtum came in. He looked better and was smiling. "I have what you need, I think," flourishing a kidney bowl overlaid with a cloth.

"Good," Bond smiled back, "and I think I have what *I* need. Put him out, Herr Doktor."

Quinn did not resist as Kirchtum rolled up his sleeve, swabbed a patch on the upper right arm and slid the hypodermic needle in. It took less than ten seconds for the man's body to relax and the head to loll over.

"He will have a good four to five hours' sleeping. You are leaving?"

"Yes, when I've made sure he can't get away once he wakes up." Bond was already busy with the straps again. "Just a precaution," he told the Herr Doktor. "One of my people should arrive here before he wakes—to make certain he gets the telephone call from his watcher, and then relays it to his source. I have to arrange that. My man will use the words, 'Ill met by moonlight.' You reply, 'Proud Titania.' Got it?"

"This is Shakespeare, the *Summer Midnight Dream,* Ja?"

"*A Midsummer Night's Dream,* Ja, Herr Doktor."

"So, Summer Midnight, Midsummer Night's, what's the difference?"

"It obviously mattered to Mr. Shakespeare. Better get it right," Bond smiled at the bearlike doctor. "Can you deal with all this?"

"Try me, Herr Bond. I deal in aces."

Five minutes later, Bond was heading back to where he had left the Saab. Within twenty he had returned to the hotel.

In his room he called Nannie to apologize for keeping them waiting. "Slight change of plan," he told her. "Just stand by. Tell Sukie. I'll be in touch soon. With luck we'll be leaving within the hour."

"What the hell's going on?" Nannie sounded peeved.

"Just stay put. Don't worry, I won't leave without you."

184

"I should jolly well think not," she snapped, banging down the receiver.

Bond smiled to himself, opened the briefcase containing the CC500 scrambler unit and attached it to the telephone. Though he was, to all intents and purposes, on his own in this situation, it was time to call for some limited assistance from the Service.

He dialed the London Regent's Park number, knowing the line would be safe now he had taken out the team at the Klinik, and asked for the duty officer, who came on the line almost straight away. After identifying himself, Bond began to issue his instructions. There were matters he wanted relayed quickly to M, and from him to the Vienna Resident. He was precise and firm, saying that there was only one way to deal with the matter—his way. If M would not—or could not—comply, then they had lost the chance, literally, of a lifetime. SPECTRE was a sitting target that only he could smash. But his instructions had to be carried out to the letter. He ended by repeating the hotel number and his room, asking for a call-back as quickly as possible.

It took just over fifteen minutes. M had okayed all the instructions and the operation was already running from Vienna. A private jet would bring in a team of three men and two girls. They would wait at Salzburg airport for Bond, who should get clearance for a private flight to Zurich on his Universal Export passport B. Bookings were made on the Pan American Flight 115 from Zurich to Miami, departing at 10:15 A.M. local time.

Bond thanked him and was about to close the line. "Predator." The duty officer stopped him, using 007's identification code name.

"Yes?"

"Private message from M."

"Go on."

"He says, 'England Expects.' Nelson, I suppose— 'England expects that every man will do his duty.'"

"Yes," Bond countered irritably. "Yes, I *do* know the quotation."

"And he says 'good luck,' sir."

Bond thanked him. He knew that he would need every ounce of luck that came his way. He unhooked the CC500 and dialed Nannie's room. "All set. We're almost ready for the off."

"About time," her voice had a small smile in it. "Where're we going?"

"Off to see the Wizard," Bond laughed without humor. "The Wonderful Wizard of Oz."

— 13 —

Good Evening,
Mr. Boldman

"JAMES?" Sukie sounded almost wheedling, as they left the hotel, lugging their suitcases. "James, you're going the wrong way. You left the Bentley in the car park to the left."

"Yes," Bond spoke quietly. "Don't tell the whole world, Sukie. We're not using the Bentley." On his way back, after parking the Saab, he had made a quick detour and used the old trick of sticking the Bentley's keys up the exhaust pipe. It was not as safe as he would have liked, but it would have to do.

"Not. . . ?" An intake of breath from Nannie.

"We have alternative transport." Bond was crisp, his voice sharp with authority. The whole of his plan to outflank Tamil Rahani and SPECTRE depended on caution and timing. For a few moments, during the drive back from the Klinik, he had even considered ditching Sukie and Nannie—leaving them in the hotel. But, unless there was a way to isolate them, it was a safer course of action to take them along with him. They had already shown their determination to remain with him anyway. Dumping them now was asking for trouble.

He led them toward the Saab, Nannie muttering something about their being unable to be of help if they didn't know what was going on.

"I hope your American visas are up to date," Bond said, once they were packed into the car and he started the engine.

"American?" Sukie's voice rose in a petulant squeak.

"Visas not okay?" He edged out of the parking place and began to negotiate the streets to take them onto the airport road.

"Of course!" Nannie cross.

"I haven't a thing to wear," Sukie said loudly.

"Jeans and a shirt, where we're going," Bond smiled as he turned onto the Innsbruck road, the *Flughafen* sign illuminated for a second in his headlights. "Another thing," he added. "Before we leave this car you'll have to stow your hardware in one of my cases. We're heading for Zurich, then flying direct to the States. I have a shielded compartment in my big case and all weapons'll have to go in there. From Zurich it'll be commercial airlines until we get to our final destination."

188

Nannie began to protest, and Bond shut her up quickly. "You both decided to stay with me on this. If you want out, then say so now and I'll have you taken back to the hotel. You can have fun going to all those Mozart concerts."

"We're coming, whatever." Nannie said firmly. "Both of us, okay, Sukie?"

"You bet your sweet—"

"As arranged, then." Bond could see the *Flughafen* signs coming up fast now. "There's a private jet on its way for us now. I shall have to spend some time with the people who're arriving on it. *That* you cannot be in on, I'm afraid. Then we take off for Zurich."

In the airport car park, Bond opened the hatchback and unzipped his folding case—which took up to four suits and an incredible amount of shirts and accessories. Q Branch had taken the brown lightweight Samsonite case apart and fitted a sturdy extra zipped compartment into the center. This pocket was shielded against all known airport surveillance and X-ray equipment, and even though it meant weapons had to travel in commercial aircraft freight compartments, Bond had found it invaluable when traveling with airlines that did not give him permission to carry a personal weapon.

"Anything you should not be carrying, ladies, please." He held out a hand while both Sukie and Nannie hoisted their skirts and unclipped identical holsters, complete with automatic pistols, from their garter belts.

In the odd light of the sodium lamps surrounding the car park, Bond could not see if there were any blushes, but he recalled the odd anomaly of Sukie's being modest, while the seemingly straitlaced Nannie had pranced around the apartment where Der Haken had died wearing the most flimsy apparel.

When the case was zipped again and returned to the luggage compartment, he ordered the girls back into the car. "Remember, you're unarmed. If anything happens either stay put or run for it. I shall be with the airport manager. As far as I can tell there's no danger, because the people who're really on my trail now have, I hope, been diverted." He said he would not be long, and then walked toward the small cluster of airport buildings.

The airport manager had been fully alerted and treated the arrival of an executive aircraft as a perfectly normal and routine matter—just as it was supposed to be. "They are about fifty miles out, and just starting their approach," he told Bond. "I gather you need some kind of room for a small conference while the aircraft is being turned around."

Bond nodded, apologizing for the inconvenience of having the airport opened at this time of night.

"Just thank heaven the weather is good," the manager gave an uncertain smile. "It's not possible at night if things close in."

190

They went out onto the apron, and Bond saw that the airport had been lit for the arrival. A few minutes later he spotted the flashing red and green lights creeping down the invisible path of the approach to the main runway. A few seconds later the little HS 125 Exec jet came hissing in over the threshold to touch down neatly, pulling up with a sharp deceleration. The pilot had obviously used Salzburg before and knew its limits.

Within a short time the aircraft, bearing a British identification number and no other markings, pulled up, guided toward its parking area by an expert "batsman" using a pair of illuminated batons.

The forward door opened and the airsteps unfolded, like old-fashioned sugar tongs. Bond did not recognize the two girls, but was glad to see that at least two of the three men who came down onto the tarmac were people he had worked with before. The most senior was a bronzed, well-honed young man called Crispin Thrush, whose experience was almost as varied as that of Bond.

The two men shook hands, and Crispin introduced him to the other members of the team as the manager led them to a small, deserted conference room, already prepared, with coffee, bottles of mineral water, and note pads set out on a circular table.

"Help yourselves." Bond looked around at the team. "I think I'll go and wash my hands, as they say." He cocked his head at Crispin, who nodded and followed him out of the room, along the passage, and finally out into the airport parking lot.

When they spoke it was with lowered voices.

"They briefed you?" Bond asked.

"Only the basics. Said you'd put the flesh on it."

"Right. You and one of the other boys take a rented Saab—the one with the couple of girls in it, over there—and go straight up to the Klinik Mozart. You've got the route?"

Thrush nodded. "They gave us that. Yes. And I was told something almost unbelievable . . ."

"Steve?"

He nodded again.

"Well, it's true. You'll find him there, sleeping off some dope the Klinik's director, Doctor Kirchtum, gave him. You'll find Kirchtum a godsend. Quinn and a couple of heavies have been holding him there . . ." He went on to explain that part of the situation—that there was some cleaning up to be done, and Quinn to be ready to take a telephone call from the KGB man watching the road for the Bentley. "When he makes his radio report, listen to him and watch him, Crispin. He's a rogue agent, and I've no need to tell you how dangerous that can be. He knows all the tricks, and I've only got his cooperation because of threats against his wife."

"They pulled Tabby in, I understand. She's stashed in one of the Rome safe houses. Gather the poor girl's a bit bemused."

"Probably doesn't believe it. He claims she had no

192

idea that he'd defected. Anyway, if the whole team'll fit into the Saab you'd better drop your two girls and the other lad off at the Goldener Hirsch." He told Crispin where the Bentley could be found, with the keys in the exhaust, and the route he wanted it to take to Paris. "If we all get a move on—ten minutes for a bit of nonsense chat in the conference room—you can get the Bentley team on their way. The car'll be spotted, so make sure you've got time to get settled into the Klinik, with Quinn awake, before the Bentley leaves. Their watcher'll take it for granted that I'm in it, with my companions, heading for Paris. That should throw them for a while."

Once the messages had been passed on, Crispin and his man were to get Steve Quinn out and on to Vienna. "Quickest way possible. The car, I should think."

There were a couple of questions and a final back-track on the plan, then Crispin reached into his jacket and pulled out a heavy, long envelope. "Tickets." He passed the envelope over. "With the Resident's com-pliments." Bond slid the papers into his breast pocket, and the pair returned, walking slowly, to the building and conference room.

They stayed there for less than fifteen minutes, drinking coffee and ad libbing a business meeting concerning an export deal in chocolate. Eventually Bond rose. "Right, ladies and gentlemen. See you outside, then."

Already he had arranged to get his party, and

their luggage, out of the Saab so that Sukie and Nannie would not even see the team that had flown in. He used some charm to get a man to assist with the luggage, and then gave the girls rapid instructions to follow him into the airport building, where the manager would be waiting.

He joined them a few minutes later, having passed on the Saab keys to Crispin and wished the new team good luck. "M's going to boil you in oil if this goes wrong," Crispin smiled at him.

Bond cocked an eyebrow, sensing the small comma of hair had fallen over his right temple. "If there's anything left of me to boil." As he said it, Bond had a strange premonition of impending disaster coming from some unsuspected source.

"VIP treatment," Sukie sounded delighted when she saw the executive jet, complete with crew and one steward. "Just like the old days with Pasquale."

Nannie simply took it in her stride. Within minutes they were buckled into their seatbelts, whining down the runway and lifting into the black hole of the night.

The steward came around with drinks and sandwiches, then discreetly left them alone.

"So where are we going, James, for the umpteenth time?" Sukie raised her glass.

"And what's more to the point, why?" Nannie sipped her uniced mineral water.

"The where is Florida. Miami first, and then onward. The why's more difficult."

194

"Try us," Nannie smiled, peering up over her granny spectacles.

"Oh, we've had a rotten apple in the barrel. Someone I trusted. He set me up, so now I've set him up, arranged a small diversion so that his people imagine we're all on the way to Paris. In reality, as you can see, we're traveling, in some style, to Zurich. From thence we go on, by courtesy of Pan American Airlines, to Miami. First class, naturally, but I suggest that we separate once we reach Zurich. So, tickets, ladies."

He opened the envelope given to him by Crispin and handed over the long blue and white folders containing the Zurich–Miami segment of the flight. The girls' were made out in their real names—The Principessa Sukie Tempesta and Miss Nannette Norrich. He held back the Providence and Boston Airlines tickets that would get them from Miami to Key West. For some reason he sensed it was better not to let them know the final destination until the last minute. He also glanced at his own ticket to check it was in the name of Mr. J. Boldman—the alias used on what was known as his "B" passport, in which he was described as a company director. All appeared to be in order.

They arranged with the captain, via the steward, to disembark separately at Zurich; to travel independently on the Pan Am flight, and to meet again by the Delta Airlines desk in the main concourse at Miami International. "Get a Skycap to take you there," Bond counseled. "I know the way, but the place is vast and you can get lost at the drop of a boarding pass. Also,

195

beware of legal panhandlers—Hare Krishna, nuns, whatever, they're—"

"Thick on the ground," completed Nannie. "We know, James, we've been to Miami before."

"Sorry. Right. We're set then. If either of you have second thoughts . . ."

"We've been over that as well. We're going to see it through." From Nannie.

"To the bitter end, James." Sukie leaned forward and covered his hand with her own. Bond nodded.

He caught sight of the girls at Zurich, having a snack in one of the splendid cafés that littered that clean and pleasant airport. Bond drank coffee and ate a croissant, then checked in for the Pan Am flight.

On the 747, Sukie and Nannie were seated right up in the front, while Bond occupied a window seat on the starboard side. Neither girl gave him a second look, and he admired the way Sukie had so quickly picked up field technique; Nannie he almost took for granted—already she had shown how good she could be.

The food was reasonable, the flight boring, the movie violent and cut to ribbons by the powers that control in-flight movies. At last, though, they landed at Miami International soon after eight in the evening, local time.

It was hot and crowded, but the girls were already at the Delta counter when he reached them.

"Okay," he greeted them. "Now we go through

Gate E, to the PBA departures." He handed them the last tickets.

"Key West?" queried Nannie.

"The 'Last Resort,' they call it," Sukie laughed. "Great, I've been there."

"Well, now's your chance. I want to arrive—"

The ping-pong of an announcement signal on the loudspeaker system interrupted him. He opened his mouth to continue, expecting it to be a routine call for some departure, but the voice mentioned the name Boldman, so he waited, listening for the repeat.

"Would Mr. James Boldman, passenger recently arrived from Zurich, go to the information desk opposite the British Airways counter for an urgent message."

Bond shrugged, "I was going to say that I wanted to arrive incognito. Well, that's my incognito. There has to be some development from my people. Wait for me."

He made his way through the crowds, pressing through lines of people with baggage waiting to check in at various airlines, finally arriving at the information desk.

A blonde with teeth in gloss white and lips in blood red batted eyelids and asked, "Can I help y'awl?"

"Message for James Boldman," he said and saw her glance behind his left shoulder and nod.

197

The voice was soft in his ear, and unmistakable, "Good evening, Mr. Boldman. How nice to see you."

Steve Quinn pressed close as Bond turned. He could feel the pistol muzzle hard against his ribs, and knew his face to be an etching of surprise.

"Hallo, nice for us to be meeting again, Mr.— what you call yourself now?—Mr. Boldman. Is this right?" Herr Doktor Kirchtum stood on the other side, his big face molded into what appeared to be a big smile of welcome.

"What. . . ?" Bond began.

"Just start walking quietly out of the exit doors over there." Quinn's smile remained, perfect. "Forget your traveling companions, and the PBA flight. We're going to Key West by a different route."

— 14 —

Frost-Free City

THE AIRCRAFT WAS VERY SILENT in flight—a low rumbling whine from the jets, and that was all. Bond, who had only managed a quick look at the plane before boarding, thought it looked like an Aérospatiale Corvette, with its distinctive long nose-probe.

The interior was sleek and luxurious—customized, as they said in the trade, with six swivel armchairs, a long central table and plush decor in blue and gold.

Below them there was darkness, only the occasional pin of light flashing in the distance, so he presumed they were now high over the Everglades, or turning to make the run to Key West across the sea.

The initial shock of finding himself flanked by

Quinn and Kirchtum had passed very quickly. In his job one learned to adapt with speed, think on the run and act accordingly; and in this situation his only option was to go along with Quinn's instructions: In fact it was his only chance of survival.

There had been a moment's hesitation after he felt the gun pressing through cloth into his flesh and saw the faces, then he obeyed, walking calmly between the two men—both big, and crowding him like a pair of cops making a discreet arrest.

Now, he thought, he was really on his own and with nothing up his sleeve. The girls had tickets to Key West, but he had told them to wait for him. They also had the luggage, and his case contained all the weapons—Nannie's two little automatics, the ASP and the steel telescopic baton.

The long black limo with tinted windows stood, parked, directly outside the exit. Kirchtum moved forward a pace to open the rear door, bent his heavy body and entered first.

"In!" Quinn prodded with the gun, almost pushing Bond into the leather-scented interior, quickly following him so that he was closely sandwiched between the two men.

The motor started before the door slammed shut, and the vehicle pulled smoothly away from the curb. Quinn had the gun out now—a small Makarov, Russian made and based on the German Walther PP series design. Bond recognized it immediately, even in the dim glow thrown into the car from the external lights dotted and sprouting from the driveways and airport access roads.

By the same light he could see the driver's head, like a large, elongated coconut, topped with a peaked cap.

Nobody spoke, and no orders were given.

The limo purred onto a slip-road leading, Bond guessed, to the airport perimeter tracks, for Quinn whispered, "Not a word, James. On your life, and May's and Moneypenny's as well." They were approaching a high chain-link fence, into which large gates were set, with a security shack, complete with two uniformed guards.

The car stopped, and there was the whine of the driver's window coming down as one of the guards approached. The driver's hand came up, clutching a fistful of IDs, and the guards said something. The nearside rear window slid down, the guard peering in, looking at the cards in his hand and then glancing in at Quinn, Bond and Kirchtum. "Okay," he said, at last, in a gravel voice. "Through the gate and wait for the guide truck."

They moved forward and stopped, lights dipped. Somewhere ahead of them there was a mighty roar as an aircraft landed, slamming on its reverse thrust so that the noise blanketed everything.

Dimmed light appeared ahead, and a small truck did a neat turn in front of them. It was painted with yellow stripes, a red light revolved on the canopy. The rear was well lit with a large *Follow Me* sign.

They moved off again, obeying the truck, driving very slowly past aircraft of all types—commercial jets, loading and unloading, big piston-engined planes, freighters, small private craft, the insignias ranging from Pan Am, British Airways and Delta to Datsun and Island City Flying Service.

Their aircraft—the one Bond thought was a Corvette—stood well apart from the main gaggle, near a cluster of hangars and buildings on the far side of the field. They pulled up so close that Bond had a moment's concern that they might even touch a wing.

For large men, Quinn and Kirchtum moved with efficient speed, like a well-drilled team, Kirchtum leaving the car almost before it had come to a standstill, and Quinn edging Bond toward the door, so that he was constantly covered from both sides.

Once out in the open, Kirchtum's hand grasped his arm like a steel trap until Quinn was out. The rest was very fast—an arm-lock and pressure, forcing Bond toward the airdoor and up the steps. He was in the cabin, with Quinn, pistol now in full view, behind him in seconds, and Kirchtum closing the door, the airsteps folding inward and the door locking with a solid clunk.

"That seat," Quinn indicated with the pistol, while Kirchtum moved in with two pairs of handcuffs, which clicked around their victim's wrists and were fitted solidly with small steel D-rings into the padded arms of the seat.

"You've done this before," Bond smiled. There was no edge in showing fear to people like this.

"A precaution." Quinn stood clear, the pistol leveled, as Kirchtum looped shackles around Bond's ankles and secured them to similar steel D-rings on the lower part of the seat. "It would be foolish to be forced to use this once we're airborne." Quinn indicated the pistol as the engines rumbled into life. Seconds later they were moving.

There had been a short wait as they taxied, in line, waiting for other airplanes to be cleared, then the little jet swung onto the runway, burst into full life and rocketed away, climbing fast.

"I apologize for the deception, James." Quinn was now relaxed and leaning back in his seat with a drink. "You see, we thought you might just possibly visit the Mozart, so we stayed prepared for that possibility—even with the torture paraphernalia on show, and the Herr Doktor looking like an unwilling victim. I admit to one serious error: I should have ordered my outside team to move in after you entered. However, these things happen. But the Herr Doktor was excellent in his role of frightened captive, I thought."

"Oscar nominee." Bond's expression did not alter. "I hope nothing nasty's going to happen to my two lady friends."

"I don't think you need bother yourself about them," Quinn smiled happily. "We sent them a message that you would not be leaving tonight. They think you're joining them at the Airport Hilton. I should imagine they're waiting there for you now. If they do get suspicious, I fear they won't be able to do much about it. You have a date in the morning—I should imagine about lunchtime—with what the good old French revolutionaries called Madame La Guillotine. I shall not be there to witness it. As I told you before, my department merely has orders to hand you over to the self-styled Colonel Rahani and his organization, SPECTRE. We take the money and see to the release of May and Moneypenny—you can trust me regarding that. They will be returned, 'unopened,' as the jargon has it, though it would be useful to interrogate Moneypenny."

"And where is all this going to take place?" Bond asked, his voice showing no concern regarding his appointment with the guillotine.

"Oh, quite near Key West. A few miles offshore. Outside the reef. Our timing isn't that brilliant, because we'll have to hole up with you until dawn. The channel through the reef is not the easiest to navigate, and we don't want to end up on a sandbar. But we'll manage. Arrangements have been made. I promised my superiors that *we* would hand you over and deal with the competition. I like to keep promises."

"Especially to the kind of masters you serve," Bond muttered. "Failure isn't exactly appreciated in the Russian service. At best you'd be demoted, or end up running exercises for trainees; at worst it would be one of those nice hospitals where they inject you with Aminazin—such a pleasant drug. Turns you into a living vegetable. I reckon that's exactly how you'll end up." He turned to Kirchtum, "You as well, Herr Doktor. How did they put the arm on you?"

The burly doctor gave a huge shrug. "The Klinik Mozart is my whole life, Herr Bond. My entire life. Some years ago we had—how do I put it?—a financial embarrassment. . . ?"

"You were broke," Bond said, placidly.

"So. Ja. Yes, broke. No funds. Friends of Mr. Quinn—the people he works for—made me a very good offer. I could carry on my work, which has always been in the interests of humanity, and they would see to the funds."

"I can guess the rest. The price was your cooperation. The odd visitor, to be kept under sedation for a while and then moved. Sometimes a body. Occasionally some surgery."

The doctor nodded sadly, "Ja. All those things. I admit that I did not expect to become involved in a situation like the present one. But Mr. Quinn tells me I shall be able to return with no blot on my professional character. Officially I am away for two days. A rest."

205

Bond laughed. "A rest? You believe that? It can only end with arrest, Herr Doktor. Either arrest, or one of Mr. Quinn's bullets. Probably the latter."

"Stop that," Quinn said sharply. "The doctor is well and truly involved. He has been of great help. He will be rewarded, and he knows it." He smiled at Kirchtum. "Mr. Bond is using an old, old trick, trying to make you doubt our intentions; attempting to drive a wedge between us. You know how clever he can be. You've seen him in action."

Again the doctor nodded. "Ja. The shooting of Vasili and Yuri was unexpectedly unfunny. That I did not like."

"But you were also clever—giving Mr. Quinn some harmless injection . . ."

"Water."

"And, presumably, following me."

"We were on your track very quickly." Quinn glanced toward the window. Outside there was still darkness. "But you changed *my* plans, I fear. My people in Paris were supposed to deal with you. It took some very fast and fancy choreography, James. But we managed."

"You did indeed." Bond swiveled his seat, leaning forward to edge his head close to the window. He thought there were lights in the distance.

"Ah," Quinn sounded pleased, "there are. Lights—Stock Island and Key West. About ten minutes to go, I imagine."

206

"And what if I make a fuss when we land?"

"You won't make a fuss."

"You're very confident."

"I have faith. Just as you had faith that I would comply because of Tabitha, I really do believe that you will do as you're told in order to secure the release of May and Moneypenny. It's the one chink in your armor, James. Always has been. Yes, you're a cold fish; ruthless. But you're also an old-fashioned English gentleman at heart. Saint George and all that. You'd give your life to save a damsel in distress, only this time we're not talking of damsels, but of an aging housekeeper, to whom you're devoted, and your Chief's personal assistant—a lady who has loved you hopelessly and from afar for years." He shook his head, smiling. "Not damsels held under spells or captured by dragons. People you *care* for in thrall to one of the dragons you hate most in all the world. You'd give your life for them. It's, unhappily, in your nature. Unhappily, did I say? I really meant happily—for us, happily."

Bond swallowed. Deep down inside he knew that Steve Quinn had played the trump card. He was quite right: 007 would go to his own death to preserve the lives of people like May and Moneypenny.

As the glitter of lights grew closer and brighter, James Bond reflected on the irony. Many times, he had put himself in jeopardy for young and beautiful women. Now, unless some miracle saved him, he was about to die for an elderly woman and a pleasant lady, whom he liked, yet could never fall in love with in a million years.

"There is another reason why you won't make a fuss." Quinn's smile, which one had to search for under the bushy beard—it did not show in his eyes—was still there. "Show him, Herr Doktor."

Kirchtum lifted a small case that lay in the magazine rack between the seats. From the case he drew out what looked like a child's space gun made of clear plastic. "Is an injection pistol." Kirchtum gave a sort of grin. "Before we land I shall fill it. Look, you can see the action." He drew back a small plunger from the rear, lifted the barrel in front of Bond's face and touched the tiny trigger—the whole thing was no more than three inches long, with a couple of inches for the butt. As he touched the trigger, a hypodermic needle appeared, fast as a piece of magician's equipment, from the muzzle. "Injection is given in 2.5 seconds." The Herr Doktor nodded gravely again. "Very quick. Also the needle is very long. Goes easily through cloth."

"You show the least sign of making a fuss, and you'll get the needle, right?"

"Instant death."

"Oh, no. Instant facsimile heart attack. You'll come back to us within half an hour, as good as new. Rahani and SPECTRE want your head. If the worst comes to the worst, then we must kill you and do the unpleasant business with a power tool. But we'd rather deliver the whole body, alive and intact. We owe Rahani several favors, and the poor man hasn't long to live. Your head is his last request, and it'll make his deathbed day to watch that clever, cruel head leave your restless body. So, you won't make a fuss."

"No fuss," Bond agreed, and a moment later the pilot came on the intercom system to ask that seatbelts be fastened and cigarettes extinguished. "We'll be landing in about four minutes," he announced.

Bond watched from the window as they dropped toward the lights. He saw buildings, water, tropical palms, roads, traffic and multicolored signs coming up to meet them.

"Interesting place, Key West," mused Quinn. "Hemingway once called it 'The poor man's St. Tropez'; Tennessee Williams lived here, and many more creative folk. President Truman established a 'Little White House' near what used to be the naval base; John F. Kennedy brought the British PM—Harold Macmillan—to visit; Cuban boat people landed here; but, long before that, it was a pirates' and wreckers' paradise. I'm told it's still a smugglers' heaven, and the United States Coast Guard operates a tight schedule out of here." They swept in over the threshold and touched down with hardly a bump.

"There's history in this airport as well," Quinn continued. "First regular United States mail flight started from here, and Key West is both the beginning and end of Highway Route One." They were rolling to a halt, turning to taxi toward a shacklike hut, with a veranda, which looked as though it had come straight off the back lot of some Hollywood company in the 1940s. Bond saw a low wall with faded lettering—*Welcome to Key West, the Only Frost-Free City in the United States.*

"And they have the most spectacular sunsets," Quinn added. "Really incredible. Pity you won't be around to see one."

The heat hit them like a furnace as they left the aircraft. Even the mild breeze was like a light wind blown from an inferno.

They had organized the departure from the jet as carefully as the boarding, leaving Bond in no doubt that—even though his hands and feet were now free—he would be unconscious very quickly if he did anything to cause suspicion. "Smile and pretend to talk," muttered Quinn, glancing toward the veranda where a dozen or so people were waiting to welcome passengers off a newly arrived PBA flight. Bond scanned faces, but saw nobody who looked remotely like a friend.

They passed through a small gate in the wall abutting the arrivals and departures shack, Quinn and Kirchtum nudging him forward toward a sleek dark automobile. They followed the same routine they had performed at Miami, and in a matter of moments,

Bond was again seated between the two men, though this time the driver was visible—young, open-necked shirt, blonde long hair. "Y'awl okay?" he asked.

"Just drive," Quinn ordered. "There's a place arranged, I understand."

"Sure thing. Git y'there in no time." He drew out onto the road, turning his head slightly, "Y'awl mind if'n I have some music playin'?"

"Go ahead. As long as it doesn't frighten the horses." Quinn was very relaxed and confident. If it had not been for Kirchtum, tense on the other side, Bond would have made a move. But the Herr Doktor was wound up like a hair trigger. He would have the hypo into 007 even if he moved quickly.

A burst of sound filled the car, a rough voice singing, tired, cynical and sad.

> There's a hole in Daddy's arm,
> Where all the money goes . . .

"Not that!" cracked Quinn.

"Ah'm sorry. I kinda like rock and roll. Rhythm and blues. Man, it's good music."

"I said not *that*."

The car went silent, the driver sullen. Bond watched the lights and signs—*South Roosevelt Blvd.* A restaurant alive with people eating—*Martha's*. Lush tropical foliage, the swish of tires, the ocean on their right; they appeared to be following a long bend tak-

211

ing them away from the Atlantic, and there were clapboard houses, white with fretted gingerbread decorations along the porches and verandas; lights flashed—*Motel; No Vacancy*. Then they turned, quite suddenly, at a sign—*Searstown*—and Bond saw they were in a large shopping area.

The car pulled up between a supermarket—the lights blazing and people still buying—and an optician's shop. Between the two there was a narrow alley.

"It's up there. Door on the right. Up above the eye place, where they sell reading glasses. Guess y'awl want me to pick you up."

"Five o'clock." Quinn spoke quietly. "In time to get to Garrison Bight at dawn."

"Y'awl goin' on a fishin' trip, then." The driver turned around and Bond saw his face for the first time. He was not a young man, as Bond had thought—or at least life had been unkind to him in his true youth, for, though he had long blond hair, half the man's face was missing, sunken in and patched with skin grafts. He must have detected shock in Bond for he looked at him straight with his one good eye and gave an unearthly grimace. "Don't you worry about me none. That's why I work for these gentlemen here. I got this brand new face in Nam, so I thought I could put it to use. Frightens the hell outa some folks."

"Five o'clock," Quinn repeated, opening the door.

The routine did not vary. They had Bond out,

along the alley, through a door and up one flight of stairs in no time.

It was a bare room. Two chairs and two beds. Curtains, a noisy air-conditioning unit, and precious little else. Again they used the handcuffs and shackles on Bond, and Kirchtum sat near him—hypo-gun in hand—while Quinn went out for food. They ate melon, some bread and ham, washing it down with mineral water. Then Quinn and Kirchtum took turns guarding Bond, who, giving himself up to the inevitable, went to sleep.

It was still just dark when Quinn shook him awake and stood over him in the little bathroom—bare and functional as the rest of the place. After ten minutes or so, with Bond trying to fight off the grogginess of travel and time, they led him downstairs.

The car was waiting, and they drove out, unnoticed by the very few who were showing signs of life at this time in the morning. The sky looked hard and gray, but Quinn said it was going to be a beautiful day, and that it was a pity Bond would not be around to sample all of it.

North Roosevelt Blvd. Then some kind of marina to their left—yachts and big powered fishing boats. Water to their right as well. Quinn pointed, "That'll be where we'll be heading. Gulf of Mexico. The island's out on the far side of the reef."

They came up to a restaurant sign—*Harbor Lights*—and hustled Bond out, along the side of the dead, sleeping restaurant and down onto the marina quayside where a tanned, tall and muscular man waited near a forty-foot powered fishing boat, complete with a high laddered and skeletal superstructure above the cabin, its engines idling.

Quinn and the captain exchanged nods, and they bundled Bond aboard, down into the narrow cabin. Once more the handcuffs and shackles went on, the motor noise rose and Bond could feel the swell as the craft started out from the quayside, cruising its way into the marina, under a bridge, and then picking up speed. Kirchtum had put away the hypo and seemed to be calm, while Quinn appeared to have joined the captain at the controls.

Five minutes out they really started to make way, the boat rolling slightly and bounding, slapping hard down into the water. Everyone was concentrating on the navigation, and Bond began to think seriously about his predicament. They had spoken of an island outside the reef, and he wondered how long it would take them. He then concentrated on the handcuffs, realizing before he even began that there was little he could do to get out of them. Houdini, he thought, would have had problems.

Then, unexpectedly, Quinn came down into the cabin. "I'm going to gag you and cover you up." He looked slightly concerned. "There's what looks like another fishing powerboat to starboard, and they appear to be in some kind of trouble. The captain says we should at least offer help. If they have a radio they could report us, and I don't want to raise any alarms. Stay still."

He pushed a handkerchief into Bond's mouth, and then tied another around it, so that for a moment he thought he would suffocate. Then, after checking the shackles, Quinn threw a blanket over him. In the darkness Bond listened.

They were slowing, rolling a little, but definitely slowing. Above, he heard the captain shouting, "Are you in trouble?" Then, a few seconds later, "Right, I'll come aboard, but I have an RV. May have to pick you up on the way back."

There was a sharp bump, as though they had made contact with the other boat, and then all hell broke loose.

Bond lost count after the first dozen shots—cracks: hand guns, he thought. Then the stutter of a machine pistol. A cry, which sounded like Kirchtum, and a number of thumps on the deck above him. Then silence, until he sensed someone nearby. The sound of bare feet descending into the cabin.

The blanket was hauled back roughly and Bond tried to turn his head, eyes widening as he saw the figure above him.

"Well, well, Master James." Nannie Norrich had her small automatic in one hand. "We do have to get you out of some scrapes, don't we?" She turned her head. "Sukie, it's okay. He's down here, trussed up and oven ready by the look of it."

Sukie appeared, also armed. She grinned appealingly. "Bondage, they call it, I believe." She began to laugh as Bond loosed off a stream of obscenities, which were completely inaudible from behind his gag.

They began to work on the handcuffs and shackles. Sukie went aloft again, returning with keys.

"I hope those idiots weren't friends of yours," said Nannie. "I'm afraid we had to deal with them."

The gag came away. "What do you mean, 'deal'?" Bond spluttered. She looked so innocent that his blood ran cold at her answer.

"I'm afraid they're dead, James. All three of them. Stone dead. But you must admit we were clever to find *you*."

216

— 15 —

The Price
For a Life

INDEED, THE CAPTAIN, Steve Quinn and Herr Doktor Kirchtum *were* dead. Stone dead, as Nannie had said, though "stone dead" was not an accurate description. They were bone dead—bone, tissue, cell, muscle, flesh and blood dead.

The captain lay on his back in the little wheelhouse—his shirt bloodied and ripped by at least two bullets that had hit him high, near the throat. Herr Doktor Kirchtum was crumpled in the stern well, his face strangely happy, his body like a beached baby whale. There was not much blood—a trickle coming from the folds of flesh, and Bond guessed he had caught his lethal wounds in the stomach. Nearby lay an Uzi machine pistol.

Steve Quinn was the worst. Obviously he had moved forward, trying to take shelter and shoot from

217

behind the superstructure. The glass around the wheelhouse and upper cabin was starred and shattered, while Quinn lay flat on his back, what was left of his head pointing toward the prow. Two, maybe three bullets, Bond thought: meticulously aimed for the head. Quinn had been thrown back against the guard rail, probably hitting the three neatly rolled life jackets and then bouncing onto the deck.

None of it was pretty, and Bond felt an odd sense of surprise that the two relatively young girls who had brought about this carnage remained buoyant, even elated, as though killing three men were like swatting flies in a kitchen. He also realized that he was suffering from a certain amount of resentment—he had taken the initiative; he had been duped by Quinn and Kirchtum; he had fallen into their quickly devised trap. Yet he had not been able to effect his own escape—the girls had rescued him, and he felt vaguely resentful about it. A peculiar reaction when he should have been very grateful.

A power fishing boat—almost identical to the one in which Bond had been held—lay alongside, rising, falling and gently bumping the boat of death. The sea was smooth, the sky turning from pearl to deep blue as the sun cleared the horizon. It was going to be a beautiful day.

They were well outside the reef, and in the far distance little low mounds of island rose from the sea.

"Well?" Nannie stood near him, looking around

218

THE PRICE FOR A LIFE

while Sukie appeared to be busying herself on their boat.

"Well what?" Bond asked flatly, his voice tinged with diffidence.

"Well, weren't we clever to find you?"

"Very." Sharp, clipped and almost angry. "Was this all necessary?"

"You mean blowing away your captors?" The expression sounded strange coming from the prim-looking Nannie Norrich. "Yes," she flushed with anger now. "Yes, very necessary. Can't you even say thank you, James? We tried to deal with it peacefully, but they opened up with that damned Uzi." She pointed toward their boat and the nasty jagged row of holes in the hull, abaft the high skeleton superstructure above the cabin. "They gave us no option."

Bond nodded, muttering his thanks. Then, "You were, indeed, *very* clever to find me. I'd like to hear more about that."

"And so you shall." Nannie had adopted a waspish attitude. "But first we really have to do something about this mess," waving a hand around her to indicate boat and bodies alike.

"What weapons're you carrying?"

"The two pistols from your case—your stuff's back at the hotel in Key West. I had to force two of the padlocks, I'm afraid—couldn't work out the combinations, and we had become fairly desperate by then."

219

"Any extra fuel around?"

She pointed, past Kirchtum's body in the stern well. "A couple of cans there. We've got three aboard our boat."

"It's got to look like a catastrophe," Bond frowned. "What's more, they mustn't find the bodies. An explosion would be best—preferably with us well out of the area. It's easy enough, but we really need some kind of fuse, and that's what we haven't got."

"We have a signal pistol—flares."

Bond nodded. "Then that's the only possible way. What's the range—about a hundred yards? You get back with Sukie. Break out the pistol and flares, I'll do what's necessary here."

She nodded, turned away and sprang lightly onto the guard rail, jumping aboard their boat and calling to Sukie.

Bond then set about the somewhat grim task, working with efficient speed, his mind still churning the facts. How *did* the girls manage to find him? How *could* they be in the right place at the right time? He needed the answers to those questions, and until they satisfied him there was no possible way he could trust either of the young women.

He searched the boat carefully, carrying everything that might be of use up onto the deck—rope, wire, boxes of fishing gear that included the ultra-strong lines used for bringing in large fish like sharks and swordfish.

220

All the weapons went overboard, except for Quinn's automatic—a prosaic Browning 9mm—and some spare clips.

Next came the grisly job of moving the bodies into the stern well. Kirchtum, being already there, only needed turning over, a task accomplished with Bond's feet; the captain's body stuck in the wheelhouse door, and he had to tug hard to get him free, while Quinn was the most difficult of all, for he had to be dragged along the narrow gap separating cabin from guard rail.

He arranged the bodies in a row, lashing them loosely together with fishing line, positioning them directly over where he knew the fuel tanks to be located. He then went forward again, gathering as much inflammable material as he could—sheets and blankets off the four bunks in the cabin, cushions, pillows and even pieces of rag. These he bundled together, well forward, weighting them with life jackets and other heavier pieces of equipment. He left one piece of coiled rope near the bodies and then transferred himself to the other boat, where Sukie and Nannie were standing close to each other—Sukie forward in the wheel house, Nannie behind her, on the steps leading down to the cabin.

"There it is. One flare pistol." Nannie held the bulbous flare projector by the muzzle.

"Plenty of flares?"

She pointed to a metal box containing a dozen or

so stumpy cartridges, each marked with their colors—red, green and illuminating. Bond picked out three of the last. "These should do us." He rapidly told them what was required, and Sukie started the engines as Nannie began to cast off all but one rope amidships.

Bond returned to Quinn's boat to make the final preparations. He dragged the rope from the bodies to the pile of material forward, secured it under the pile and gently played it out back to the stern well, laying it alongside the inlets to the fuel tanks.

He then went forward again carrying one of the two cans of emergency fuel, saturating the material at the front of the boat and running plenty of the liquid over the rope, shuffling backward toward the bodies and fuel caps.

Last he opened the second can, dowsed the bodies in fuel and unscrewed the main fuel cap, inserting the saturated rope, lowering it into the tank. Then he turned and yelled "Stand by!" to the girls, ran from the stern well, mounted the guard rail and was aboard the other boat just as Nannie let go of the one rope that attached the vessels one to the other. Sukie slowly eased the engines open, and they pulled away, gently turning stern-on to the boat from which he had been rescued.

Bond positioned himself aft of the superstructure, slid a flare into the pistol, checked the wind and watched the gap slowly widen between the two craft.

222

At around eighty yards he raised the pistol high and fired an illuminating flare, using a low, flat trajectory. The flare hissed right across the bow of the other boat, but by the time he realized it was a miss, Bond had already reloaded and taken up another position.

This time, the fizzing white flare performed a perfect arc, leaving a thick stream of white smoke behind it, to land in the bow of the other craft. There was a second's pause before the material ignited with a small whumph, and Bond saw the flames being carried straight along the rope fuse toward the fuel tanks, above which the bodies lay.

"Give her full power and weave as much as possible!" Bond shouted to Sukie. The engine note rose, bow lifting, almost before he had completed the order.

Rapidly they bounced away from the blazing fishing boat.

The bodies caught fire, the stern well sending up a crimson flame and then a dense cloud of black smoke. They were a good mile and a half away when the fuel tanks went up—a great roaring explosion with a dark red center, ripping the boat and, he presumed, the bodies apart in a ferocious fireball.

It was the end—just the smoke, the scarlet center of flame, a rising cascade of debris, then nothing. The water appeared to boil around what little remained of the powerful fishing boat, then settled, steamed for a few seconds, and flattened. The shock waves hit the rear of their boat a second or two after the explosion. There was a slight burn on the wind, which they all felt on their cheeks.

At three miles there was nothing to be seen, but Bond remained leaning against the superstructure, gazing in the direction of what had been a small and violent inferno.

"Coffee?" Nannie asked.

"Depends how long we're staying at sea."

"We hired this thing for a day's fishing," she grinned. "I don't think we should make it too obvious."

"No, we'll even have to try to fish. Sukie okay at the wheel?"

Sukie Tempesta turned, nodded and smiled.

"She's an expert." Nannie gestured toward the steps down under the wheelhouse. "There's coffee on."

"And I want to hear how you managed to find me." Bond gave her a steady, suspicious look.

"I told you. I was minding you, James." They were seated in the cramped cabin, he on one bunk facing Nannie, who sat on the other. They both nursed mugs of coffee, and the power boat rolled and thudded against the sea. Sukie had reduced power, and they appeared to be performing a series of gentle, wide circles. "When members of Norrich Universal Bodyguards take it upon themselves to look after you, you get looked after." She had her long legs tucked under her on the bunk, and had unpinned her hair so that it fell, dark and thick, to her shoulders, giving her face an almost elfin look, and somehow making the gray eyes softer and very interesting.

Take care, Bond thought, this lady has to explain herself, and she had better be convincing.

"So I got looked after." He did not smile.

She explained that as soon as he was paged at Miami International, she had told Sukie to stay with the luggage while she followed at a discreet distance. "I had plenty of cover—you know that, the place was crowded—but I saw the routine and I'm experienced enough to know when a client is being pulled."

"But they took me away by car."

"Yes, I had its number, though, and made two quick telephone calls—my little NUB has a small branch here, and they put a trace on the limo. I said I'd call them back if I needed assistance. I then called the flight planning office."

"Resourceful lady."

"James, in this game you have to be. Apart from the scheduled flights to Key West there was one private Exec jet that had a filed flight plan. I took down the details—"

"Which were?"

"Company called Société pour la Promotion de l'Ecologie et de la Civilisation."

SPEC, Bond thought. SPEC. SPECTRE.

"We had about six minutes to catch the PBA flight

to Key West, so I gambled we'd make it just before the private flight."

"You also gambled on my being on board the SPEC jet."

She nodded, "True, but you were. If you hadn't been on it, I would have had egg on my face. However, we were in, and off the aircraft a good five minutes before you came along. I even had time to hire a car, send Sukie to the best hotel in town and follow you to that shopping center in Searstown."

"And then what?"

"I hung around," she paused, not looking at him. "To be honest, I didn't really know what to do, then, like a small miracle, the big bearded guy came out and went straight to the telephone booth. I was only a few paces away, but—in spite of the spectacles—I've got good eyesight. I watched him punch out a number and talk for a while. He went to the supermarket and I took his place in the booth and dialed the number—he called the Harbor Lights Restaurant."

She had got a map and guide with the little rented VW ("They said a small car would be best"), so the Harbor Lights was easy enough to find. "As soon as I got inside I realized it was a fishing and yachting people's paradise—full of bronzed, muscular men who rented boats, and themselves to sail them. I just asked around. One guy—the one who went up in smoke just now—let it slip that he had been hired for an early start. He'd had a bit to drink and even told me what time he was leaving, *with three passengers*."

226

"So you hired another powered fishing boat."

"Right. Told the captain I didn't need help—knowing Sukie could really navigate the trickiest of waters blindfolded and with her hands tied. He took me down to this boat, made a pass, got rebuked, showed me the charts, told me about the currents, the channels—which are not easy—talked about the reef, the islands and the 'drop-off' into the Gulf of Mexico, eighteen miles out, and gave me the keys."

"So you went back to Sukie at the hotel . . ."

"Pored over the charts half the night, got down to Garrison Bight early and were outside the reef when your boat came out. We shadowed at a safe distance for a while, and then overtook, just out of sight, watching you on the radar. Positioned ourselves near enough to your course, stopped engines and started firing distress flares. You know the rest."

"You tried to take her by reason, but they opened up with the Uzi."

"To their cost." She cocked her head, and gave a sigh. "Lord, I'm tired."

"You're not alone—and what about Sukie?"

"She seems happy enough. Always is with boats." She put down the empty coffee mug, her hand moving to her shirt, slowly starting to undo the buttons. "I really think I'd like to lie down, James. Would you like to lie down with me?"

"What if we hit a squall? We'll be thrown all over the place." Bond leaned forward to kiss her gently on the mouth.

"I'd rather meet a swell." Her arms came up around his neck, drawing him toward her.

Later, she said that she'd rarely been thanked so well for saving somebody's life.

"You should do it again sometime." Bond kissed her, running one hand over her naked body.

"Why not now?" asked Nannie with an implike grin. "It seems a fair price for a life."

— 16 —

Going Down Tonight

"As far as I can tell, there are three islands, outside the reef, that are privately owned, with some kind of building on them." Sukie's finger roamed around the chart of waters in the Key West vicinity.

It was early afternoon and they had hoved to, with fishing lines out. So far four large red snapper had come their way, but nothing big—no sharks, no swordfish.

"This one here," Sukie indicated an island just outside the reef, within easy distance of Key West, "is owned by the man who initially built the hotel we're booked into. There's another to the north, and this one," her finger circled a largish patch of land, "just on the shelf, before you reach the drop-off— the edge of the Continental Shelf, where the depth goes straight from eight hundred to eighteen hundred.

Great fishing water around the drop-off. There've also been treasure seekers by the dozen in the area." She prodded the island on the map. "Anyway, it looked very much as though that was where you were heading."

Bond peered closer to see the name. "Shark Island," he said aloud. "How cozy."

"Someone appears to think so. I asked around the hotel last night. A couple of years ago a man who called himself Rainey—Tarquin Rainey—bought the place. The boy at the hotel is from an old Key West family, and knows all the gossip. Says this fellow Rainey isn't seen by people—mystery man; arrives by private jet and gets ferried out to Shark Island by helicopter or a launch, which usually stays out there. He's also a bit of a go-getter. People who build on the islands usually take a lot of time; there's always difficulty getting the materials taken out, but Rainey had his place up in the space of one summer. The second summer saw the island landscaped—he's got tropical trees, gardens, the lot. They're very impressed, the people in Key West, and it takes a great deal to impress them—particularly as they claim to be a republic: the Conch Republic, pronounced 'Konk.'"

"*Nobody's* seen him?" Bond asked, knowing that the alias Tarquin Rainey was just too good to be true. It had to be Tamil Rahani, which meant Shark Island was SPECTRE property.

"Not officially, no. There are folk who've had a

glimpse, of course—at a distance. Nobody's encouraged to get near him, though. Apparently some boats have approached Shark Island and been warned away—politely, but very firmly—by large men in fast motorboats."

"Mmmmm." Bond thought for a few minutes, then asked Sukie if she could navigate to within a mile or so at night.

"If the charts are accurate, yes. It'll be slow going, but it's possible. When did you want to go?"

"I thought perhaps tonight." Bond looked steadily from Sukie to Nannie. "If that was where I was being taken, then it's really only courteous for me to call on Mr. Rainey at the earliest possible opportunity."

The girls looked dubious.

"I think we should head back to Garrison Bight now. See if you can keep up the boat hire for a couple of days; then let me get myself one or two bits and pieces I'm going to need, have a look around Key West—see and be seen—and sail about two in the morning. I won't put you in danger, *that* I promise. You simply wait offshore. If I don't return by a certain time, then you get the hell out of it and come back tomorrow night."

"Okay by me." Sukie got to her feet.

Nannie just nodded. She had been quiet all day since they had come back on deck—silent, with many warm glances in Bond's direction.

231

"Right. Let's get the lines hauled in. We sail at two. In the meantime there's a great deal to be done."

The local police were at Garrison Bight, checking on the boat hired by Steve Quinn. There had been a report from another powerboat that had seen a plume of smoke, and from a Navy helicopter that had spotted wreckage, and sighted *Prospero*—the name of the boat hired by Nannie—some miles from the spot. They had seen the chopper, an hour or so after Quinn's boat had exploded—even waved to it, knowing they were well distanced from Quinn's vessel.

Nannie went ashore and talked to the law, while Sukie stayed in sight on deck and Bond remained in the cabin. It took around half an hour, and Nannie returned, all smiles, saying she had charmed the pants off the cops and hired the boat for a week.

"I hope we're not going to need it that long," Bond grimaced.

"Better safe than sorry, as we Nannies are supposed to say." She poked her tongue out before adding, "Master James."

"I've had enough of that little joke, thank you." He sounded genuinely irritated. "Now, where are we staying? Where's my luggage?"

"Only one place to stay in Key West," Sukie joined in. "The Pier House Hotel. You get a wonderful view of the famous sunset from there."

"I've a lot to do before sunset," Bond said sharply.

232

"The sooner we get to this—what's it called, Pier House?—the better."

As they set off in the hired VW, Bond suddenly felt very naked without his own weapons. He sat next to Nannie, with Sukie squeezed into the back giving an occasional running commentary, having been to the island before.

The place, to Bond, seemed an odd mixture of down-market resort tackiness, sudden snatches of great beauty and large patches of luxury that spelled money. It was hot, palm trees shimmered and moved in the light breeze, and they passed numerous clapboard gingerbread houses, which had a satisfying, pleasing look to them, most of them bright, well-painted and kept in good order, their yards and gardens bright with the color of sub-tropical flowers.

The odd thing was that you could see several of these houses, in perfect condition, but next to run-down places, or even rubbish dumps. The sidewalks were also either in fine order or cracked, broken or nearly nonexistent.

At an intersection, they had to wait for an extraordinary-looking train—a kind of model railroad engine, built onto what appeared to be a diesel-powered jeep, pulled a series of cars, full of people, sitting interested under striped awnings.

"The Conch Train," Sukie informed them. "That's the way tourists get to see Key West."

Bond could hear the driver, all done out in blue overalls and peaked cap, going through a litany of the sights and history as the train wound its way around the island.

They finally turned into a long street that was a mixture of wood and concrete and appeared to house a mile or so of jewelry, tourist junk and art shops, together with great batches of restaurants, which looked very prosperous indeed.

"Duval," announced Sukie, giving them the name of the street and commenting on restaurants and places of interest as they went. "It goes right down to the ocean—to our hotel in fact—and it's great at night. There, see, that's the famous Fast Buck Freddie's Department Store; Antonia's, a great Italian restaurant; and here comes Sloppy Joe's Bar. They say it was Ernest Hemingway's favorite haunt when he lived here.

There was no doubt that Hemingway had lived in Key West. Even if Bond had not known it through reading *To Have and Have Not* he would certainly be apprised of the fact now, for many of the shops had souvenir T-shirts or drawings of Hemingway, while Sloppy Joe's Bar proclaimed the fact loudly, from an inn sign and a tall painted legend on the wall.

The sidewalks were crowded, and the order of dress ranged from straight casual to casual bizarre—the shortest of shorts, the most ragged of cutoffs, T-shirts with weird slogans decorating chests and bosoms: *I owe, I owe, so off to work I go;* and *Sex Tuition Here: First Lesson Free.*

As they reached the bottom of Duval, Bond saw what he was looking for and made a note that it was within very quick walking distance of the hotel, the grounds of which were on their right.

"You're already registered, and your luggage is in your suite," Nannie told him, as she parked the car, and, together, the girls hustled him through the main reception area—all light, friendliness and bamboo—through doors into an enclosed courtyard. In the center a fountain played among flowers and a tall wooden statue of a naked woman. Above, large fans revolved silently, sending a downdraft of cool air.

He followed them down a passage and out into the garden, with its twisting flower-bordered pathways, a pool deck to the left, and beyond that more wood and bamboo: a line of bars and restaurants ran beside a small beach—a pier (after which the hotel was named) held out over the water on big wooden piles.

The whole building appeared to be U-shaped—the gardens, pool and beach located in the center of the U. They entered the main hotel again at the far side of the pool, and went into an elevator and up one floor.

There were two suites, next to each other. "We're sharing," Sukie said, inserting her key into one of the doors. "But you're right next to us, James, in case there's anything we can do for you." For the first time since they had met, Bond thought he could detect an invitation in Sukie's voice. He certainly saw a small angry flash of fire in Nannie's eyes. Could it be that the pair were fighting over him?

"What's the plan?" Nannie asked, a shade sharply.

"Where's the best place to watch this incredible sunset you've been telling me about?"

She allowed him a smile. "The deck outside the Havana Docks Bar—or so they tell me."

"And what's the witching hour?"

"Around six."

"The bar's in the hotel?"

"Right over there," she waved a hand, vaguely, in the direction from which they had come. "Up above the restaurants. Right out toward the sea."

"Meet you both there at six, then." Bond smiled, turned the key in his door and disappeared into what proved to be a pleasant and functional—if not altogether luxurious—suite.

The pair of briefcases and his special Samsonite folding case stood in the middle of the room, and it took Bond less than ten minutes to organize his unpacking. He felt better with the ASP back on his person and the concealable operations baton hidden away under his jacket.

He checked the rooms carefully, made certain the window catches were secure, then quietly opened the door. The corridor was deserted. Silently he closed the door, making his way quickly to the elevator, then back down into the gardens, through an exit to the car park he had noted on the way through, and then out into the hot and humid air.

At the far end of the parking lot stood a low building—the Pier House Market—access to which could be gained from either the hotel or Front Street.

Bond walked straight through, pausing for a moment to look at the fruits and meats on sale, then made his way onto Front Street, turning right and crossing the cracked and lumpy road, walking fast to the corner of Duval. He passed the shop he really wanted to visit, and went on until he found a small male boutique where he bought some faded jeans, a T-shirt without any tasteless slogan and a pair of soft loafers. When in Rome, he thought. Finally he chose an overpriced short linen jacket. For people in Bond's job some kind of jacket or blouse was always necessary, if only to hide the hardware.

He came out of the boutique, turned and made his way back to the place he had spotted from the car. It had an open front decorated with a dummy clad in scuba gear, and the legend above the big walk-in front read *Reef Plunderers' Diving Emporium*.

The bearded, tanned salesman started to try to sell him a three-and-a-half-hour snorkeling trip on board a dive boat called, predictably, *Reef Plunderer II*, but Bond knew exactly what he wanted.

"Captain Jack knows all the best places to dive

along the reef," the salesman protested, wasting his breath.

"I want a wet suit, snorkeling mask, knife, flippers, undersea torch, and a shoulder bag for the lot," Bond told him, using the soft yet commanding tone that always demanded attention.

The salesman looked at Bond, took in the physique under the lightweight suit and the hard look in the icy blue eyes. "Yes siree. Sure. Right," he said, leading the way to the rear of the shop. "Gonna cost a ransom, but you sure know what y'awl're after."

"That's right." Bond did not allow his voice to rise above the almost whispering softness.

"Right," the salesman repeated. He was dressed to look like an experienced man of the sea, with a striped T-shirt and jeans. A gold ring hung, piratically rather than fashionably, from one ear. He gave Bond another sidelong look and began to collect equipment from the back of the store. It took ten minutes before Bond was completely satisfied with the purchases—adding a belt with a waterproof zipper bag to his list, and producing a Platinum Amex Card, made out in the name of James Boldman, with which to pay.

"Guess I'll have to just run a check on this, sir, Mr. Boldman."

"You don't *have* to, and you know it." Bond's eyes held less humanity in them than small chips of ice. "But if you're about to make telephone calls, I'm going to stand next to you, right?"

"Right. Right." The pirate salesman repeated, leading the way to a tiny office at the rear of the store. "Yes sir-bub. Yes siree." He picked up the telephone and dialed the Amex clearance number. They okayed the card in five seconds flat. It took ten minutes for the purchases to be stashed into the shoulder bag, and as he left Bond put his mouth very close to the pierced ear with the ring in it. "Tell you what," he began. "I'm a stranger in town, but now you know my name."

"Sure." The pirate gave him a trapped look.

"If anyone else gets to know I've been here, excepting you, Amex and myself, I shall personally return, cut that ring from your ear and then do the same job on your nose, followed by a more vital organ." He dropped his hand, fist clenched, so that it lay level with the pirate's crotch. "You understand me? I mean it," and he certainly sounded and looked as though he did.

The pirate knew the score. He was a good, hardworking man, but recognized the type of character Bond was projecting.

"I already forgot your name, Mr. . . . er . . . Mr. . . . ."

"Keep it like that," and Bond was off, out of the shop and into the street, walking briskly, then slowly to the more leisurely pace of those around him.

Back in his suite he lugged the CC500 from its briefcase, hooked it to the telephone and put in a quick call to London, not waiting for a response, merely giving them his exact location and saying he would be in touch as soon as the job was completed.

"It's going down tonight," he finished. "If I'm not in touch within forty-eight hours, look for Shark Island, off Key West. Repeat, it's going down tonight."

It was a very apt phrase, he thought as he changed into his newly acquired jeans, shirt, loafers and jacket. The ASP and baton were in place, so he did not feel naked, but, he thought, surveying himself in the mirror, he would blend in nicely with the tourist scene.

"Going down tonight," he said softly to himself, then left to join the girls on the Havana Docks Bar deck.

— 17 —

Shark Island

THE DECK IN FRONT of the Havana Docks Bar at the Pier House was made of wooden planks, raised on several levels and strategically decorated with metal chairs and tables—the whole thing gave one a feeling of being on board a ship at anchor.

Globe lights on poles stood at intervals along the heavy wooden guard rail, and at sunset in Key West it was *the* place to be.

The deck was crowded and the lights had come on, attracting the night bugs that swarmed around the globes. Inside, someone was playing a piano —"Mood Indigo"—and the rails were lined with camera-hung tourists, eager to capture the sunset for posterity.

As the clear sky turned to a deeper navy blue, an

occasional speedboat crossed in front of the hotel, while a light aircraft buzzed a wide circuit, its lights flashing. All was chatter, and to the left, along the wide Mallory Square, which fronted the ocean, jugglers, conjurers, fire eaters and acrobats performed among a crush of people. It was the same on every fine night—a celebration of the day's end and a look toward the pleasures night might bring.

A "Sunset Cruise" boat slid by, so loaded that it looked as if some macabre immigrant ship were leaving Key West, its passengers escaping peril—political or natural.

James Bond, sitting at a table, looking out to sea and the two dark green humps that were Tank and Wisteria islands, close inshore, thought that if he had any sense he would be on a boat or plane moving out. He was in no doubt of the peril close at hand; that Tarquin Rainey was "Colonel" Tamil Rahani, Blofeld's successor; that Shark Island, with its recently built house and landscaping, was his old enemy SPECTRE's new headquarters; and that this could well be his last chance to smash the organization for good and all.

In the warm and pleasant surroundings, Bond's mental antenna reached out and recorded the signals of malevolence nearby. As far as he and SPECTRE were concerned it was a question of smash or be smashed.

"Isn't this absolutely super?" laughed Sukie.

"There really is nothing like it in the whole world." It was unclear whether she was talking about the huge shrimp they were eating, with that very special delicious tangy and hot red sauce, the calypso daiquiris they drank or the truly beautiful view.

Bond sipped his daiquiri, took a bite of a shrimp and muttered, "Super," unconvincingly.

"It *is* incredible." Nannie squeezed his hand. "Just look at that sky."

The sun appeared to become larger as it dropped slowly behind Wisteria Island—larger and more crimson, throwing a huge patch of blood-red light across the sky, the great fire of color hitting the water, spreading as though an invisible artist were controlling a giant laser display.

"God's own light show," said Bond, now also mesmerized by the extraordinary beauty of a spectacular sunset on the southernmost tip of the United States.

Above them, a United States Customs helicopter clattered on its way, running from south to north, red and green lights twinkling on and off as it turned, heading toward the naval air station. Bond wondered if SPECTRE had become involved in the huge drug traffic that was reported to pass into America by this route—landing the drugs on isolated sections of the Florida Keys, to be taken inland and distributed. The Navy and Customs kept a very close eye on places like Key West.

A great cheer went up—echoed from the hundreds of people farther up the coastline on Mallory Square—as the sun finally appeared to plunge into the sea, filling the whole sky with deep scarlet for a couple of minutes before the velvet darkness took over.

"So what's the deal, James?" Nannie asked in almost a whisper.

All three of them lowered their heads over the plates of shrimp, conspirators sharing a secret with seafood.

Bond spoke low, saying that those who were after him were, first, almost certainly on Shark Island, and, second, they *knew* he had arrived in Key West. "I want them to think that I'm taking my time," he murmured. "They could well act tonight, here, at the Pier House. That's why we've got to make the first move."

He told them that, until midnight at least, he wanted all three of them to stay visible. "We'll stroll out into town, get a good dinner and come back to the hotel. Then I want us out—separately. We must each go our own way. You're not to use the car, and you'll both have to keep an eye out for anyone on your tails. Nannie, you're trained in this kind of thing, so give Sukie the benefit of your experience. Brief her; tell her the best way to do the trick. I have my own plans. But the most important thing is that we all meet at Garrison Bight, aboard the *Prospero*, around one in the morning, okay?"

The two girls nodded, and Bond noticed a small

concerned furrow take shape between Nannie's eyes. "What then?" she asked.

"Has Sukie looked at the charts?"

"Yes, it's not the easiest trip by night." Sukie's eyes showed nothing, neither fear nor elation. "It's a challenge, though. The sandbars are not well marked and we'll have to show a certain amount of light to begin with. Once we're beyond the reef it's not too bad."

"Just get me to within a mile of the island." Bond gave her a hard look, and his voice was edged with authority.

They finished their drinks and the shrimp, rose and began to saunter casually from the deck. At the door to the bar, Bond paused, asking the girls to wait for a moment as he went back to look over the rails, down into the sea. Earlier he had noticed the hotel's little pull-start speedboat making trips just off the beach. It was now neatly tied up between the big wooden piles that held this section of the hotel out over the water. Smiling to himself, he rejoined the girls, and they went through the bar—the pianist was now playing "Bewitched"—and down toward the reception area. They passed along the wooden walkway running alongside the hotel's crowded eating places—the Pier House Restaurant, the Beach Club Bar and Pete's Raw Bar ("Doing a raw-ring trade," Sukie said, and they all groaned).

A small dance floor had been set up across from

the bars, on the beach, and a three-man combo had started to pound out rhythms for the cognoscenti; the paths were lit by small lamps, and people were still swimming, diving into the floodlit pool, laughing with pleasure. It was fairyland magic: certainly fairyland when one took a close look at the waiters.

Outside, the streets were as crowded as they had been in midafternoon, and few people appeared to have changed from their leisure clothes into anything more formal.

They strolled, arms linked—one girl on each side of Bond—down Duval, looking into windows and peering into the restaurants, which all seemed to be booked solidly for the evening.

Halfway along the street a crowd stood in front of the light gray, Victorian English–looking church staring across the road where, in front of Fast Buck Freddie's Department Store, half a dozen kids were breakdancing to the music of a ghetto-blaster.

Eventually, they retraced their footsteps and found themselves in front of Claire, a restaurant that, while busy, looked exceptionally good. They walked in through a small garden to the maître d', who hovered by a tall desk, in the open air outside the main restaurant.

"Boldman," lied Bond with conviction. "Party of three. Eight o'clock."

The maître d' consulted his book, looked troubled and asked when the booking had been made.

"Yesterday evening," Bond kept up the fantasy, and prayed that the girls would not let him down by giggling.

"There seems to be some error, Mr. Boldman," the bemused man said, a shade too firmly for Bond's liking.

"I reserved the table specially. It's the only night we can make it this week. I spoke to a young man, last night, and he assured me I had the table."

"Just one moment, sir." The maître d' disappeared into the restaurant and they could see he was deep in an agitated conversation with one of the waiters. Finally he came out all smiles. "You're lucky, sir. We've had an unexpected cancellation . . ."

"Not lucky," Bond clenched his jaw. "We had a table *reserved*. We're simply getting our table."

"Certainly, sir," and they were shown into a pleasant room decorated in white, to a corner table where Bond took a seat with his back to the wall and a good view of the entrance.

The tablecloths were made of paper, and there were packets of crayons beside each plate, so that guests could create their own art—perhaps the restaurant's owners were still hoping Picasso would arrive and pay the bill with the tablecloth.

Nannie leaned forward. "I haven't spotted anyone. Are we being watched."

"Oh, yes." He opened the large menu, with a smile. "Two of them. Possibly three. At least two,

247

working each side of the street. A guy in a yellow shirt and jeans, tall, black and with a lot of rings on his fingers. The other's a little runt, dark trousers, a white shirt, deep tan and a tattoo on his left arm—mermaid being indecent with a swordfish by the look of it. He's across the street now." Bond doodled on the paper tablecloth, drawing a skull and crossed bones. Nannie had sketched something vaguely obscene, in red.

"Got 'em." Nannie also consulted her menu.

"And the possible third?" asked Sukie.

"An old blue Buick. Big fellow at the wheel, alone and cruising. Not easy to tell, but he's been up and down the street a lot—so have others—but he was the only one who didn't seem to take any interest in people on the sidewalks. I'd say he was the backup. They're around, so watch out for them."

A waiter appeared and they all made the same decision about food—conch chowder, the Thai beef salad and, inevitably, Key Lime pie. They drank a California champagne, which slightly offended Bond's palate. They talked constantly, keeping off the immediate business in hand. Eventually, when the waiter went off with the bill and the credit card, Bond told them to be wary. "I want you all there, on board and with nobody on your backs, by one."

They nodded, Bond signed the account and within a couple of minutes they were out on the street again, walking west toward the Front Street intersection. The black man with the yellow shirt kept well back on the other side of the street, and the little tattooed man let them pass him, then overtook them and let then pass again before they got back to the Pier House.

The blue Buick had cruised by twice, and was parked outside the Lobster House, almost opposite the main entrance to the Pier House. "They have us well staked out," Bond murmured as they crossed the street and walked up the drive to the main entrance, where they all made a great show of saying goodnight.

Bond was taking no chances. The moment he got to his room he checked the old but well-tried alarm signals he had left behind. The slivers of matchstick were still in place, wedged into the doors of the clothes cupboards, while the threads on the drawers were unbroken.

He looked at the similar traps left on his luggage. Everything was intact. Now was the time to move. It was barely ten-thirty, but he wanted to get out and running as quickly as possible. He doubted that SPECTRE's surveillance team would expect anyone to make a move before the early hours. Nor had he let either of the girls know that he had quietly slipped the spare set of charts from the *Prospero* inside his jacket before leaving the fishing boat that afternoon.

249

He now spread them out on the round glass table in the center of his living room and began to study the course from Garrison Bight to Shark Island, making notes on headings, the dangerous sections of sandbar, and other hazards, as he ran a thick pencil line along the route. When he was satisfied that he had all the compass bearings correct, and a very good idea of how he could guide a boat to within safe distance of the island, Bond began to dress for action.

He took a light cotton black rollneck from his case, peeled off the T-shirt and wriggled into it. The jeans were replaced by a pair of black slacks, which he always packed—on a duty journey or holiday. Next, he spread out the wide belt that had been so useful when Der Haken had him locked up in Salzburg.

He removed the Q Branch Toolkit and checked the contents, spreading everything out on the table and paying special attention to the small explosive charges and their electronic connectors, adding to them another four small flat packets of plastique explosive, each no larger than a stick of chewing gum. These he took from the false bottom of his second briefcase, together with four short lengths of fuse, some extra-thin electric wire, half a dozen tiny detonators, a miniature pinlight torch, not much larger than the filter of a cigarette—and one other very important item. All these things would fit neatly into the inner pockets of the belt.

250

Together the explosives would not dispose of an entire building, but they could be useful with things like locks or door hinges. He secured all the equipment and then buckled on the belt, threading it through the loops on his trousers, before opening up the shoulder bag in which he had stowed the wet suit and snorkeling equipment.

Sweating a little, he struggled into the wet suit, and once comfortable clipped the knife into place on the belt he had bought with the suit. The ASP, two spare magazines, the charts and the baton went into the waterproof pouch, already threaded onto the belt, leaving flippers, mask, underwater torch and snorkel in the shoulder bag. Bond then prepared to make his exit from Key West.

He remained inside his wing of the hotel for as long as possible. There was still a great deal of action going on in the bars, restaurant and makeshift dance floor laid out on the beach, and he finally emerged through one of the exits on the ocean side of these festivities.

Squatting with his back against the wall, Bond unzipped the shoulder bag and pulled on the flippers, then slowly edged himself toward the water. The noise, music and laughter behind him were loud as he climbed over the short stretch of rock that marked the righthand boundary of the hotel bathing area. He washed the mask out, slipped it over the upper part of his face, grasped the torch, adjusted the snorkel and slid into the water, going straight down and swimming gently around the metal shark guard that ran in a wide circle to protect swimmers using the hotel beach. It took a good ten minutes for him to find the long, thick wooden piles under the Havana Docks Bar deck, but he surfaced only a few feet from where the motorboat he had seen earlier was tied up.

Any noise he made clambering aboard would not be heard from above, or on the beach, and once inside the neat little craft, he quickly used the torch to check the fuel gauges. The beach staff was efficient and the tank had been filled, presumably ready for the next morning's work.

He cast off and used his hands to maneuver the speedboat from under the pier, then allowed it to drift, occasionally guiding it with the flat of his hand in the water, heading north, into the Gulf of Mexico, silently passing the Standard Oil Company pier, which he had seen from the Havana Docks.

He allowed the boat to drift a good mile out before switching on the riding lights and moving aft to prime and start the motor. It fired at the first pull, and he had to scramble quickly forward to swing himself behind the wheel, one hand on the throttle. As he opened up, glancing down at the small luminous dial of the compass, Bond mentally thanked the Pier House for the care it took in keeping the boat in order.

252

Minutes later, he was cruising carefully around the coast, fumbling with the pouch to pull out the charts and take his first visual fix.

He could not risk !etting the speedboat run at anywhere near its full speed, but within ten minutes he had spotted the exit point from Garrison Bight, and was able to begin negotiating the tricky sandbars, watching his heading and the chart, cruising slowly, occasionally feeling the shallow draft of the boat touch the sand. Twenty minutes later he cleared the reef and set course for Shark Island.

The night was clear, and the moon was up, but Bond still had to watch speed and strain his eyes into the dark stretch of water ahead. Ten minutes; then another ten, before he caught a glimpse of lights. Less than five minutes after the first sighting, he cut the engine, drifting in. The long dark slice of land stood out against the horizon, twinkling with lights from buildings he could see clearly, set among trees. He leaned over, washed out his mask again, took up the torch and, for the second time that night, dropped into the sea.

He remained on the surface for a while, judging that he was around a mile offshore. Then he heard the thrum of engines and saw a small craft rounding the island, to his left, searching the waters with a powerful spotlight—Tamil Rahani's regular patrol, he thought. There would be at least two boats like this keeping up a constant vigil—someone had said peo-

ple were warned off during the daylight, and, knowing SPECTRE's thoroughness, Bond assumed they
would not halt the patrols when the sun went down.

He took in air and went deep, swimming steadily
but not flat out, conserving energy against any panic
moment that might come.

On the way in, he surfaced twice, and the second
time told him that they had found the speedboat.
Their craft had stopped and voices drifted over the
water. He had around half a mile to go now, and his
main worry was the possibility of meeting sharks—
the island would not be named after the creatures if
they were not known to haunt the vicinity.

His luck held—at least until he came suddenly
against the heavy wire mesh of an antishark barrier
around sixty yards from the beach. Clinging to the
strong metal, he could see the island's lights clearly—
from the bright, large windows in the long, high
house, to the floodlights in the grounds. Looking
back he saw the spotlight from the patrol boat and
heard its engine rise again. They were coming to look
for him.

He heaved himself up onto the metal bar that
topped the protective fence. One flipper caught, awk-
wardly, in the mesh and he lost a few precious seconds disentangling himself before finally lowering his
body into the water on the far side.

Again, he went down deep, swimming a little
more strongly—faster—now he was almost there. He

254

had gone about ten yards when instinct told him there was danger: something close. Then he felt the bump, jarring his ribs, throwing him to one side.

Bond turned his head and saw, swimming beside him, as though keeping station with him, the ugly wicked snout of a bull shark. The protective fence was not there to keep the creatures out, but to make sure that an island guard of sharks remained close inshore—the favorite hunting ground of the dangerous bull shark.

The shark had bumped him, but, so far, had not attempted to turn and attack, which probably meant either that it was well-fed or that it had not yet sized up Bond as an enemy or the chef's special on today's menu. He knew his only salvation was to remain calm, not to antagonize the shark, and certainly not to knowingly transmit fear—though he was probably doing that at the moment.

Still keeping pace with the shark, he allowed his right hand to go down to the knife handle, his fingers closing around it, ready to unsheath and use the weapon at a second's notice. He remembered also that on no account must he drop his legs: If he did that, the shark would know in an instant that he was prey, and the bull shark could move like a racing boat. The most dangerous moment lay ahead, and not very far ahead, when he reached the beach— there he would be at his most vulnerable.

The shark continued to keep station, then, as

Bond felt the first touch of sand under his belly, as
the water became shallow, he was aware of the shark
moving, dropping back. He swam on until his flippers
began to churn sand, and, in that moment, he knew
the shark was behind, probably even beginning to
build up speed for the strike.

Later Bond thought he had seldom moved as
quickly in water. He gave a mighty push, sending his
body upward, bringing his encumbered feet down,
then splashing, racing for the beach, in an odd splay-
footed, leg-raising, hopping run dictated by the suit
and flippers.

He got to the surf, and then the sand, in one great
leap, and as he hit, rolled to the left: just in time, for
the bull shark's snout—jaws wide and snapping—
broke through the surf, missing him by inches.

Bond continued to roll, trying to propel himself
up the beach, for he had heard of bull sharks coming
right out of the water to attack. Six feet up, he lay still,
the first danger past—panting, feeling his stomach
reel with a stab of fear.

Quickly, his subconscious told him to move. He
was *on* the island, and heaven alone knew with what
other guardians SPECTRE had surrounded its headquarters and its dying leader. He kicked off the flippers and ran forward, crouched, to the first line of
palms and undergrowth. There, he squatted again to
take stock.

256

Before doing anything, he dumped the mask and snorkel with the flippers, pushing them under the bushes. The air was balmy and the sweet smell of night-blooming tropical flowers came to his nostrils like a magic potion. As he crouched and listened he could detect no noises or movement coming from the grounds, which were—now he was close—well-lit and obviously laid out with paths, small water gardens, trees, statues and flowers. There was a low murmur of voices coming from the house—though far away, inside—and the house itself was something that had to be seen to be believed. It was built like a pyramid, lifted high above the ground on great polished steel girders. He could make out three stories, each surrounded by a metal balcony running around the whole of the building.

Behind all of the balconies were large picture windows, some of them partly open, others with curtains drawn, and atop the whole pyramid, a forest of communications aerials stretched up like some avant-garde skeletal sculpture.

Gently, he reached down, opened the waterproof pouch and drew out the ASP, cocking it and taking the safety off. He was breathing normally now, and using the trees, darker patches of the gardens and the statues for cover, Bond inched his way silently toward this vast, slab-sided modern pyramid.

As he got closer, he saw there were several ways

into the place—a giant spiral staircase running up through the center, and three zigzagging sets of metal steps, one to each side, which rose from one terraced balcony to the next.

He crossed the final piece of open ground, standing to listen for a moment. The voices had stopped; he thought he could hear the patrol boat, far out to sea. Nothing else.

With great care, James Bond began to climb the open zigzagging stairs to the first level, his feet noiselessly touching the fretted metal, his body to the left to leave his right hand, and the ASP, ready for instant use. At the top, standing on the first terrace, he waited, head cocked. Just ahead of him there was a large sliding picture window, the curtains only partially drawn and one section of the window open.

Moving so that he covered all points of the compass around him, Bond crossed to the window, peering in. He could not believe what he saw, almost speaking his thoughts out loud—"First time lucky."

The room was white and splendidly decorated, with glass tables, white soft armchairs, and what appeared to be excellent original paintings on its walls, a deep pile white carpet covering the floor. But the central feature was a large, comfortable, customized bed—a king-sized sickbed, with controls on a panel at the head, switches and buttons that could, obviously, adjust any part of the bed, from head to foot,

258

to suit the patient who now lay in it, propped up with silk pillows, his eyes closed in sleep and his head turned to one side.

In spite of the now shrunken face, the skin a parchment pallor, Bond recognized the man immediately. On their previous meetings, Tamil Rahani had been smooth, short, dapper and attractive, in a military fashion. Now, he was a shadow of his former self—the heir to the Blofeld fortune, and the organization, SPECTRE, reduced to this human doll, swamped by the seductive luxury of a high-tech bed.

Bond slid the window open and stepped inside, moving like a cat to the end of the bed, gazing down on the man who controlled his greatest enemies.

Now I can have him, he thought. Now, why not? Kill him now and you may not ruin SPECTRE, but at least you'll decapitate it—just as its leader wants you decapitated.

Taking a deep breath, Bond raised the ASP. He was only a few steps from Rahani's head. One squeeze of the trigger and it would be obliterated, and, with luck and cunning, he could be away—hiding up in the grounds—until he found a method of getting off the island.

He began to squeeze the trigger, and as he did so thought he felt a small gust of air on the back of his head.

"I don't think so, James. We've brought you too

far to let you do what God's going to do soon enough." The voice came from behind him.

"Just drop the gun, James. Drop it, or you'll be dead before you can even move."

He was stunned by the voice. The ASP fell, with a noisy thump, to the floor and Tamil Rahani stirred and groaned in his sleep.

"Okay, you can turn around now."

Bond turned to look at Nannie Norrich, who stood in the window, an Uzi machine pistol tucked into her lithesome hip.

— 18 —

Madame Awaits

"I'M SORRY IT HAD TO BE like this, James. You lived up to your reputation. Every girl should have one." The gray eyes were as cold as the North Sea in December, and the words meant nothing.

"Not as sorry as I am." Bond allowed himself a smile that neither the muzzle of the Uzi nor Nannie Norrich deserved. "You and Sukie, eh? You really did take me in. Is it private enterprise, or do you both work for one of the organizations?"

She replied flatly, any feelings she might have had well under control, "Not Sukie, James. Sukie's for real, and, at the moment, she's out for a few hours, in bed at the Pier House. I slipped her what the old gumshoe movies would call a Mickey Finn—a *very* strong one. We had coffee after we left you. Coffee on room service, and I provided an added service of my own. You'll be well gone by the time she wakes up. If she does wake up."

Bond glanced at the bed. The shrunken figure of Tamil Rahani had not moved. Time. He needed time. Time, luck and possibly some fast talking. None of them were easily obtainable commodities. He tried to be casual. "Originally, a Mickey Finn was a laxative for horses. Did you know that?"

She took no notice. "You look like a black Kermit the Frog in that gear, James. Doesn't suit you, so—very slowly—I want you to take it off."

Bond shrugged. "If you say so."

"I do, and please don't be fooled. The tiniest move and I'll have no compunction about taking your legs off with this." The muzzle of the Uzi twitched. "Don't worry if you're naked under the wet suit. Remember I've seen it all before."

There were no options. Slowly, and with a certain amount of difficulty, Bond began to divest himself of the wet suit. As he did so, he tried to talk, picking questions with care.

"You *really* did have me fooled, Nannie. After all you saved me several times."

"More than you know." Her voice level and without emotion. "That was my job—or, at least, the job I said that I'd try to do."

"You disintegrated the German—what was his

name? Conrad Tempel?—on the road to Strasbourg?"

"Oh, yes—and there were a couple before then who had latched onto you. I dealt with them. On the boat to Ostend."

Bond nodded, acknowledging that he knew about the men on the ferry. "And Cordova—'The Rat,' the 'Poison Dwarf'?"

"Guilty."

"The hoods in the Renault?"

"Took me a little by surprise. You helped a great deal, James. Quinn was a thorn in the flesh, but you helped again. I was simply your guardian angel. That was the job."

He finally pulled off the wet suit, standing there in the slacks and the cotton rollneck. "What about Der Haken? The mad cop."

She gave a glacial smile. "I had some help there. My own private panic button—Der Haken was briefed; he thought I was a go-between for himself and SPECTRE. Colonel Rahani had given me the benefit of the doubt and sent in the heavy mob. They wanted to take you then, but the colonel let me carry on—though there was a penalty clause: My head was on the block if I lost you after that. And I nearly did, because I was responsible for the vampire bat. Lucky for you that Sukie came along to save you when she did. But her arrival gave *me* a hard time with SPEC-

263

TRE. They've been experimenting with the beasts here. It was meant to give you rabies. You were a sort of guinea pig, and the plan was to get you to Shark Island before the symptoms started to become apparent. The colonel wants your head, but he was quite content to watch you die in agony before they shortened you—as they say." She moved the Uzi again. "Let's have you against the wall, James. The standard position, feet apart, arms stretched. We don't want to find you're carrying any nasty little toys, do we?"

She frisked him expertly, and then began to remove his belt. It was the action of a trained expert, and something Bond had dreaded. "Dangerous things, belts," she said, undoing the buckle, then unthreading it from the loops. "Oh, yes. This one especially. Very cunning." She had obviously detected the Toolkit.

"If SPECTRE has someone like you on the payroll, Nannie, why bother with a charade like this competition—the Head Hunt?"

"I'm not," she said, curtly. "Not on the payroll, I mean. I entered the competition as a freelance. I've done odd bits of work for them before, so we came to an arrangement. They put me on a retainer, and I stand to get only a percentage of the prize money if I win—which I have done. The colonel has great faith in me. He saw it as a way of saving money."

264

As though he had heard talk of himself, the bundle that was Tamil Rahani, on the bed, stirred. "Who is it? What . . . Who?" The voice, so commanding, confident and firm the last time Bond had heard SPECTRE's chief speak, was now as much of a husk as the body.

"It's me, Colonel Rahani." Nannie's voice stood to attention.

"The Norrich girl?"

"Nannie, yes. I've brought a present for you."

"Help . . . sit up . . ." Rahani croaked.

"I can't at the moment. But I'll press the bell."

Bond, hands splayed against the wall, leaning forward, heard her move, but knew there was no chance of his taking any precipitate action. Nannie was fast and good with weapons at the best of times. Now, with her quarry here in the room, she would be *very* itchy with her trigger finger.

"You can stand up now, James. Slowly," she said a couple of seconds later.

He pushed himself from the wall.

"Turn around—slowly—with your arms stretched out and feet apart, then lean back against the wall."

Bond did as he was told, regaining a complete view of the room just as the door to his right opened.

The hoods who entered first both had guns in their hands.

"Relax," Nannie said softly. "I've brought him."

They were the usual SPECTRE gorillas—one fair-haired, the other balding, but both big, muscular men with wary eyes and cautious, quick movements. The fair one smiled. "Oh, good. Well done, Miss Norrich," his English laced with a slight Scandinavian accent. The bald one merely nodded.

They were followed by a short man, dressed casually in white shirt and trousers, his face distorted by the right corner of his mouth, which seemed permanently twisted toward the right ear.

"Dr. McConnell," Nannie acknowledged him.

"Aye, so it's you, Mistress Norrich. Ye've brought yon man the colonel's always raving about, then?" His face reminded Bond of a bizarre ventriloquial dummy when he spoke, in what was almost a bad stage Scottish accent. A tall, butch-looking nurse plodded in his wake—big, raw-boned, with flaxen hair: the kind of nurse Bond thought would not have been out of place among those who worked in the Nazi concentration camps during World War II.

"So, how's ma patient, then?" McConnell stood by the bed.

"I think he wants to see the present I've brought for him, Doctor." Nannie's eyes never left Bond. Now she had him, she was taking no chances.

The doctor gave a signal to the nurse, who moved toward the white bedside table. The nurse picked up a flat, black control box—attached to an electric cable that snaked under the bed—the size of a man's wallet. She pressed one of the buttons and the bed-head began to angle upward, raising Tamil Rahani into a sitting position. The electronic mechanism made no more than a mild whirring noise.

"There," the smallest hint of glee in Nannie's voice. "I said I'd do it, Colonel Rahani, and I did. Mr. James Bond, at your service."

There was a tired, wheezing cackle from Rahani as his eyes focused. "An eye for an eye, Mr. Bond. Apart from the fact that SPECTRE has wanted you dead for more years than either of us would care to recall, I have a personal score to settle with you."

"Nice to see you in such a bad way," Bond spat out the words.

"Ah!" It was meant to be some kind of laugh. "Yes, Bond. The last time we met, you caused me to jump for my life. I didn't know then that I was jumping to my death. The bad landing I suffered then jarred my spine. In turn this set in motion the incurable disease from which I am now dying. As you've personally caused the downfall of previous leaders of SPECTRE and decimated the Blofeld family, I regard it as a duty, as well as a personal privilege, to see you wiped from the face of the earth—hence the little contest." He was rapidly running out of steam, each spoken word seeming to tire him. "A contest that was a gamble with the odds in SPECTRE's favor, for we took on Miss Norrich, a tried and true operator."

"And you manipulated other contestants," Bond said grimly. "The kidnapping, I mean. I trust . . ."

"Oh, the delightful Scottish lady, and the famous Miss Moneypenny. You trust. . . ?"

"I think that's enough talking, Colonel." Dr. Mc-Connell came closer to the bed.

"No . . . no . . ." Then, weaker still, "I want to see him depart this life before I go."

"Then ye will, Colonel." The doctor bent over the bed. "Ye'll have to rest a while first, though."

Almost in a whisper, Rahani tried to speak with Bond, "You said you trust . . ."

"I trust both ladies are safe, and that, for once, SPECTRE will be honorable and see they are returned in exchange for my head."

"They are both here. Safe. They will be freed the moment your head is severed from your body." Rahani seemed to shrivel even more as his head sank back onto the pillows.

For a second Bond relived the last time he had seen the man—over the Swiss lake, strong, tough, outclassed but leaping from an airship to escape Bond's victory.

The doctor looked around at the hoods, "Is everything prepared? For the—er—the execution?" He did not even glance at Bond.

"We've been ready for a long time." The fair man gave his toothy smile again. "Everything's in order."

The doctor nodded. "The colonel hasn't got long, I fear. A day, maybe two. I have to give him medication now, and he will sleep for about three hours. Can you do it then?"

"Whenever," the balding hood nodded, then gave Bond a hard look. He had stone eyes, the color of granite and twice as indifferent.

The doctor signaled to the nurse and she busied herself preparing an injection. "Give the colonel an hour, he'll no be disturbed by being moved then. In an hour ye can move the bed into the . . . what d'ye call it? The execution chamber?"

"Good a name as any," the fair man said. "You want us to take Bond up?" he added, addressing Nannie.

"You touch him and you're dead," Nannie sounded as though she meant it. "I know the way. Just give me the keys."

"I have a request." Inside, Bond felt the first pangs of fear, but his voice was steady, even commanding.

"Yes," Nannie, diffident.

"I know it'll make little difference, but I'd like to be sure about May and Moneypenny."

Nannie looked at the two hoods. The fair one

nodded. "They're in the other two cells. Next to the death cell."

Bond could not help giving a wry smile. "SPEC-TRE made certain this place contained all modern conveniences when it was designed."

"Oh, they had you in mind," the fair hood grinn-ed. "You, and several other people." Then, to Nan-nie, "You can manage him by yourself? You're sure?"

"I got him here, didn't I? I lured him . . ."

"But we had to give you a hand with the Austrian cops."

"A temporary matter. Yes, I can manage him, Fin. Don't worry about that. If he gives me any trou-ble I'll take his legs off. The doc can no doubt patch him up for the headechtomy."

From the bed, where he was administering the injection, McConnell gave a throaty chuckle. "I like it, Mistress Norrich—headechtomy, I like it verra much."

"Which is more than can be said for me," Bond sounded very cool. At the back of his mind he was already doing some calculations. The mathematics of escape.

The doctor chuckled again, "If ye want tae get a head, get a Nannie, eh?"

"Let's go." Nannie came quite near to prodding Bond with the Uzi. "Hands *above* the head, fingers linked, arms straight. Go for the door. Move."

270

MADAME AWAITS

Bond walked forward, passing through the door to find himself in a curving passage, deep pile carpet under his feet, the decor changing from white to a sky blue. The passage, he reckoned, ran around the entire story, and was probably identical to others on the floors above. The great house on Shark Island, though externally constructed as a pyramid, appeared to have a circular core.

At intervals along the passage there were alcoves, Norman in style, each containing some objet d'art. These alone reflected the wealth amassed by SPECTRE over the years, for he recognized at least two Picabias, a Duchamp, a Dali and a Jackson Pollock. Fitting, he thought, that SPECTRE should invest money in surrealist artists.

Finally they came to a set of elevator doors—brushed steel, curved like the wall itself. Nannie commanded him to take up the hands-on-wall position again while she summoned the elevator, which arrived as soundlessly as the doors slid open. Everything appeared to have been constructed in a manner that made silence obligatory.

She ushered him into the circular cage of the elevator. The doors closed and he could hardly tell if they were moving up or down—deciding that up was the only possible way they could go. Seconds later the doors opened again, this time onto a very different kind of passage—bare, with walls that looked like plain brick and a floor that gave the impression of being made of flagstones, though no noise came from treading on them.

As the elevator disappeared, Bond could see that they were in a very small area of the second story, for the curved passage was blocked off at either end.

"The retaining area," Nannie explained. "You want to see the hostages? Okay, move left."

He did so, and she stopped him in front of a door that could have been part of a movie set, yet it was real—black metal, with a heavy lock and a tiny Judas squint. "Be my guest." Nannie waved the Uzi toward the squint.

From what he could see, the interior was comfortable enough—a somewhat spartan bedroom, on the bed of which lay May, asleep, comfortable, her chest rising and falling and her face relaxed.

"I understand they've been kept under sedation— only mild though." He thought he detected a glimmer of compassion in her voice. "They take only a second or two to be wakened for meals."

She ushered him on to a similar door, and through the squint he saw Moneypenny on a similar bed, relaxed and apparently sleeping like May.

Bond drew back and nodded.

"I'll take you to your final resting place, then, James." Any compassion had disappeared, and they went back the way they had come, this time stopping not before a door but in front of an electronic numeral pad set into the wall.

Nannie again made him take up a safe position against the wall as she tapped out a code on the numbered buttons. A section of wall slid back, and Bond was ordered forward. This time his heart and stomach turned over.

They entered a large, bare room. One wall was taken up by a row of deep comfortable chairs, like exclusive theater seats. There was a medical table and a hospital gurney trolley, but the centerpiece, lit from above by large spots, was far from surrealistic: a full-sized, very real guillotine.

Bond's first reaction was that it seemed smaller than he had expected, but that was probably due to all the French Revolution movies, which tended to show the instrument as a blade sliding down very high, grooved posts. This instrument stood barely eight feet in height, making it look like a model of all the Hollywood representations he had seen.

There was no doubt that it would do the job, though, for everything was there, from the stockslike fitment for head and hands at the bottom—with a neat, almost hygienic, plastic oblong box set to catch the dismembered head and hands—to the angled blade, firmly set at the top, between the posts. Even at a distance it was clear that it was razor sharp.

A vegetable—a large cabbage, he thought—had

273

been jammed into the hole for the head, and Nannie, in a fast and precise movement, stepped forward and touched some kind of trigger on one of the upright posts.

He did not even see the blade fall, it came down so fast. The cabbage was sliced neatly in two and there was a heavy thud as the blade settled. The whole thing was macabre and unnerving.

"In a couple of hours or so," Nannie said, brightly.

He nodded, knowing what she meant, realizing that, unless he could pull off some kind of miraculous escape, he would very soon have no head with which to nod.

She allowed him to stand for a minute to take in the scene, then pointed him toward a cell door, similar to the ones in the passage, but at the far side of the chamber, directly in line with the guillotine.

"They've done it quite well, really," Nannie almost sparkled. "The first thing you'll see, when they bring you out, will be Madame La Guillotine." She gave a little laugh, "And the last thing also. They'll do you proud, though, James. I understand that Fin is to do the honors, and he's been instructed to wear full evening dress. It'll be a classy experience."

"How many've received invitations?"

"Well, I suppose there're only about thirty-five people on the whole island—in Shark House, as they

274

call this place. Some, the communications people and guards, will be working. Ten possibly—thirteen if you count me, and should the colonel command that the hostages be present, which is not likely—" She stopped, abruptly, realizing that he could well have asked the question as a means to discover how many men and women SPECTRE had stationed on this remote island off the American mainland—which he had indeed intended.

Quickly, though, she regained her composure. It did not matter if he knew or not, for there was only one possible end to the proceedings—the blade thudding down and decapitating James Bond, separating head from body in the fraction of a second.

"Into the cell," she said quietly. "Enough is enough." Then, as he passed through the door, "I suppose I should ask if you have any last request?"

Bond turned and smiled, "Oh, most certainly, Nannie, but you're in no condition to supply it."

She shook her head, "I'm afraid not, my dear James. You've had that already—and very pleasant it was. You might even be pleased to hear that Sukie was furious. She's absolutely crazy about you, incidentally. I should have brought her along. She would have gladly complied."

"I was going to ask you about Sukie."

"What about her?"

"Why haven't you killed her? You're a pro. You

know the form. *I* would never have left someone like Sukie lying around, even in a drugged stupor. I'd have made sure she was silenced for good and all."

"It's quite possible that I have killed her. The dosage was near lethal." Nannie's voice dropped slightly—sadly. "But you're quite right, James. I should have made certain. There's no room for sentiment in our business. But . . . well, I suppose I held back slightly. We've been very close over the years, and I've always managed to hide my darker side from her. You need someone to like you, when you do this kind of thing: You need to be loved, or don't you find that? You know, when I was at school with Sukie— before I discovered what sex I was, if you follow me—I was in love with her. She's been good to me, but you're right. When we've finished with you, I shall go back and make sure she's not around anymore. She's certainly no danger to me at the moment."

"And how did you manage to engineer that meeting—between Sukie and myself?"

Nannie gave a little puff of laughter. "That really was an accident. I was playing it very much by ear. Knew where you were—we stuck a homer on your Bentley. I had it done on the boat. Sukie really did insist on making that part of the journey alone, and you *really* saved her from a fate worse than death. I was going to set up something, depending where you happened to stay, because I knew you were heading toward Rome, as she was. It's funny, but the pair of you played right into my hands. Now, any further thoughts?"

"Last requests?"

"Yes."

Bond shrugged, "I have simple tastes, Nannie. I also know when I'm beaten. I'll have a plate of scrambled eggs and a bottle of Taittinger, the '73 if that's possible."

"In my experience, anything's possible with SPECTRE. I'll see what I can do," and she was gone, the cell door slamming shut and the heavy thump of the key in the lock. The cell was a simple bare room, but for a small metal bed, covered with one blanket.

Bond waited for a moment before going to the door. The flap over the Judas squint was closed, but he would have to be quick and careful. The silence produced in this place was against him, and someone could be outside the door very quietly without his even knowing.

Slowly, Bond undid the waistband of his slacks. Very rarely did he leave things to chance these days. Certainly, Nannie had removed his belt and found Q Branch's Toolkit—the spare one, which was the special extra piece of equipment he had taken from his briefcase, back at the Pier House, and the *only* secret he had fitted inside the belt.

277

The black slacks were also made by Q Branch, and contained screened hidden compartments stitched—well-nigh undetectable—into the waistband. It took him just over a minute to remove the Toolkit and other objects from their secure hiding places. At least he knew there was a fair chance of fixing the cell door so that he could get as far as the execution chamber. After that—who knew?

He reckoned half an hour before they would bring the food. So, within thirty minutes, he must at least establish that he could open the cell door. For the second time in a matter of days he went to work with the pick-locks.

Oddly, the cell lock was simple—a straightforward mortise that could be manipulated with ease by two of the picks. He had it open, and closed again, in less than five minutes.

Opening it a second time, he pushed at the cell door and walked out into the execution chamber—eerie, with the guillotine standing, sinister, in the center.

This, he knew, would have to be a reconnaissance, and when he got to the main door, Bond discovered he could find it only because he knew roughly where it was located. The thing was wholly electronic and appeared to be part of the wall itself. If he got the explosives in the correct place he might just do it, but finding the right position to blow the electronic locks

278

would be a matter of luck more than judgment. It was then that he went back to the cell, locking the door behind him, pushing the Toolkit and other items under the blanket on the bed, depressed by the knowledge that blowing the execution chamber door was a gamble with odds of around ninety to one *against.*

In the next twenty minutes, he racked his brains in an attempt to come to some resolution—even thinking of destroying the guillotine itself, yet realizing that this would be a hopeless act of folly, and a waste of good explosives. They would still have him—and there was more than one way of separating a man from his head.

The food arrived, carried by Nannie, with the balding hood in attendance, his hands almost white-knuckled on the Uzi.

"I said nothing was impossible for SPECTRE." Nannie did not smile as she indicated the Taittinger.

Bond simply nodded, and they left.

As the cell door was closing, however, he picked up one tiny morsel of hope. "The old man's sleeping. We're going to bring him through now," he heard the balding hood say.

Rahani was to be brought up in good time, so that he could wake from his medication already in position. As long as the nurse did not stay with him, Bond might just do it. The idea now formed, whole and desperate, in his mind as he addressed himself to the scrambled eggs—which he rated four out of a possible ten—and the champagne, which was superb, '73 having been an excellent year.

As he was completing this, possibly, final treat of his life, he thought he could hear sounds from the other side of the door. He put his ear hard against the metal, straining to catch the slightest sound, then, almost by intuition, knew there was somebody approaching the door.

Swiftly he stretched himself on the bed, ears still concentrating, so that he was 90 percent sure that he heard the Judas squint move back and then into place again.

He counted off five minutes, then unearthed the Toolkit, leaving the explosives and detonators hidden for the time being.

For the second time, Bond went to work on the lock, and when the door swung open he found the chamber in darkness, but for the glow of a bedside lamp from which he could just see the electronically operated bed of SPECTRE's leader, Tamil Rahani.

He crossed the chamber and, sure enough, Rahani lay there, silent and sleeping. Bond touched the control box that operated the various mechanisms of the bed, found the wire that led below the mattress, and followed it under the bed. What he saw gave him hope, and he crossed back to the cell to bring Toolkit, explosives and the pinlight torch.

280

He slid quickly, on his back, under the bed, and in the darkness sought out the small electronic sensor box that operated the bed-head, moving it up and down to raise and lower Rahani.

The cable from the control box ran to a main switching box, bolted more or less centrally onto the underside of this luxurious piece of furniture, from which a power lead was carefully laid out to a mains plug in the wall. From the switching box, various wires ran to the sensors that operated the head, foot and differing angles of tilt. He was interested in those that connected the switching box to the bed-head sensor. Stretching forward, Bond quietly turned off the power switch in the wall, and then began to work on the slim wires that joined the main box to the bed-head sensor.

First he cut them and trimmed off about half an inch of their plastic coating. Then he collected every piece of plastic explosive he had managed to bring in. This he molded to the edge of the sensor, finally inserting an electronic detonator, its two wires hanging loose, and short, from the plastique.

All that remained now was to plait the wires, as before, only this time adding a third wire to each pair—the wires from the detonator. In the Toolkit there was a minute roll of insulating tape, no wider than a single book match. It took a little time, but he finally insulated one set of wires from the others, thereby making sure that no bare wire could be touched by somebody moving the bed.

Last, he gathered all the items used from the Toolkit, turned on the mains power again, returned to the cell, locked the door with the picks, and once more hid the Toolkit.

If all went well, the relatively small amount of explosive would be detonated the moment anyone pressed the button to raise the bed-head. When—and he had to admit *if*—the thing worked, he would have to move like lightning. But that would have to be played almost literally on the fly. He could only wait and hope.

It seemed like an eternity, but quite suddenly, there was the clunk of the key in the cell door. The fair hood called Fin stood there, in full evening dress and white gloves. Behind, and to his right, the balding hood—also in tails—carried a heavy silver dish. They were going to do this in style, Bond thought. His head would be presented to the dying Tamil Rahani on a silver charger, just as in all the old legends and myths.

Nannie Norrich appeared from behind the balding man, and for the first time Bond saw her, under the glare of the lights, as she probably was in reality. She wore a long dark dress, her hair loose and face overpainted, with makeup so that it looked more like a tartish mask than the face of the charming girl he thought he had known.

Her smile was a reflection of horrible perversity. "Madame La Guillotine awaits you, James Bond," she said. He squared his shoulders and stepped into the chamber, quickly taking in the whole scene, and the positions of everybody there.

The sliding doors were open, and he saw what he had missed before—a small shutter in the wall next to them. The shutter was open to reveal a button combination lock that was a replica of the one in the passage.

Two more big men had joined the party—standing just inside the door, each with the familiar stone face, one carrying a handgun, the other an Uzi.

Another pair—each with a handgun—were placed near Rahani's bed, as was Dr. McConnell and his nurse.

"She awaits you," Nannie prompted, and Bond took a further step into the room. It hasn't worked, he thought, then heard Rahani's voice, weak and thin from the bed. "See . . ." he whined. "Must see. Raise me up." And again, stronger, "Raise me up!"

Bond's eyes flickered around the group again, and the nurse reached for the bed's control box.

He saw, as if in closeup, her finger press down on the button that would raise the bed-head. Then hell and confusion burst about the room.

— 19 —

Death and
Destruction

FOR A FEW SECONDS, Bond thought he was
blind, deaf and, possibly, dead. He was aware of a
burning eruption of flame from the direction of
Tamil Rahani's bed. Then the flash and heat seared
his eyeballs, and it was as though somebody had
clapped cupped hands, hard, over his ears. He could
not be certain he had even heard an explosion,
though he was aware of the impact of heat and the
great blast of scorching air pushing him backward.

Time stood terrifyingly still, so that—once he realized he could see again, and move—everything took
on a dreamlike quality, and the actions of all concerned appeared to be telescoped into slow motion.
His brain, though, took in the fact that, in reality,
events were moving at high speed; also, in the fore-

front of his mind two things were repeated, over and over—survive, and save May and Moneypenny.

What he saw, in that split second of gathering his thoughts, was the remains of Rahani's bed blazing in the far corner to his right. There was nothing left of Rahani himself and, at first sight, Bond thought most of SPECTRE's leader's remains had been scattered, together with pieces of the bed, over the doctor, the nurse and the pair of hoods who had been standing close to the explosion.

All of them appeared to be oddly decorated. It took Bond a second to realize that what he saw was, in fact, partly the remains of Rahani and partly the remains of those standing near. He was aware of the doctor suddenly keeling over, pitching into the fire that had been the center of the bed; the nurse stood, stock still, her head back, clothes ripped from her body, which was covered in wounds. From her mouth came a ghastly shriek, lasting only for a second before she also fell toward the fire.

The two hoods who had been near their leader were moving, but not of their own volition. One was minus most of his clothes and part of his face, and he seemed to have been lifted up and hurled toward the center of the room, toward the guillotine. The other was also in midair, one arm flapping, half-severed, as he was hurled toward the man with the Uzi, stationed by the door.

This latter guard seemed to be alive, though shocked, for the blast—always unpredictable in any explosion—had knocked him back against the door, his arm jerking forward, hand releasing the Uzi so that it skated across the floor to land just in front of the guillotine, on the side opposite Bond.

The other door guard appeared to be unhurt, but dazed, his hand limp, clutching his pistol.

The hood who had lost part of his face let go of his pistol, which now slid, spinning like a small curling stone on slick ice—heading straight toward Bond.

It was at that moment he realized that, in anticipation of the explosion, he had stepped back into the cell as the nurse reached for the control box. In spite of the ringing in his ears, and the dazzle of his eyes, Bond had been saved any real damage from the blast. Automatically, still not able to see or hear properly, he had stepped out of the cell again.

Fin, the balding man with the silver salver and Nannie were scattered, blown in three different directions and only just—like Bond himself—beginning to react.

He seemed to be looking at the automatic pistol sliding toward him like a man mesmerized. Then he moved, flinging himself at the weapon, a tick of time before Nannie's brain registered the same idea.

He was on his belly, hand grasping the pistol, rolling, firing as he rolled—first at the remaining guard

286

near the door, then at Fin and the balding man. Two rounds apiece, in the approved Service fashion.

He heard the shots as tiny pops in his ears, and knew he had scored with each round—the guard by the door spinning backward; Fin's white evening shirt suddenly patterned with blood; the balding man clutching his stomach, a surprised look on his face as he sat, splay-legged, on the floor.

Bond swiveled, looking for Nannie, and realized that she was doing the only thing possible—making a dive for the Uzi on the far side of the guillotine. She was taking the shortest route, her body flat on the ground, arms reaching above the retaining stocks at the bottom of the instrument of death.

He saw her hands close on the weapon just as he flung himself toward the guillotine, lifting his arm and striking the projecting lever set into the nearest upright post—the lever that Nannie had herself used to demonstrate the diabolical machine.

Even through his deafness, Bond heard the horrific thud and the awful scream as the blade sliced through Nannie's arms, just below the shoulders. He was conscious of the spurting blood, the continued screaming and the fact that the fire, where Rahani's bed had been, was getting worse, pouring out thick, dark smoke.

He paused only to grab at the Uzi and shake off the pair of detached arms, the hands of which remained clamped around the weapon. It took two hard shakes to free them from the machine pistol. Then he was outside in the passageway, which was also rapidly filling with smoke.

Turning, Bond looked at the numerical electronic locking pad on the wall. At first sight it seemed to be a simple series of numbered buttons, but then he saw the bottom row, which contained red buttons marked *Time Lock.* There was a small strip of printed instructions below it—*Press Time button. Press Close. When doors shut press number of hours required. Then press Time button again. Doors will remain inoperable until period of time set has elapsed.*

His fingers stabbed out—*Time . . . Close.* The doors slid shut. Then, again—*Two . . . Four . . . Time.* Everyone in the execution chamber was either dead or dying anyway. The action of putting the doors on a twenty-four-hour time lock just might hold back the fire. Now, he thought, for the hostages.

As he ran for the cell containing May, alarm bells began to ring, and by now Bond could hear them well enough. Either the fire had set them off, or someone still with strength left had activated them from inside the death chamber.

He reached the door of the first cell, looking around wildly for any sign of a key. There were no keys, so standing well to one side, Bond fired a burst from the Uzi, not at the metal lock but at the topmost hinge and the area into which it was set. Bullets whined and ricocheted around the passage, but they also threw out great splinters of wood, and, with pleasure, Bond saw the door sag as the area around the hinge gave way. He turned the Uzi onto the lower hinge, gave it two fast bursts and leaped to one side as the slab of metal detached itself from the wall, hesitated, then fell heavily to one side.

May cowered back on her bed, eyes wide with fear, looking as though she was attempting to push her body through the wall.

"It's okay, May! It's me!" he yelled, and she gasped out, "Mr. James! Oh, my God, Mr. James!"

"Just hang on there," Bond shouted at her, realizing he was raising his voice too high—a result of the temporary deafness caused by the explosion. "Hang on while I get Moneypenny. Don't come out into the passage until I tell you!"

"Mr. James, how did. . . ?" she began, but he was away, up the passage to the next cell door, where he repeated the process with the Uzi.

When the door fell, he found Moneypenny in an attitude similar to that in which he had discovered May.

"It's okay, Moneypenny." He was breathless and the passage appeared to be filling with even more smoke. "It's okay. It's the white knight come to take you off on the pommel of his saddle, or something like that."

She looked gray with fear and was shaking badly.

"James! Oh, James. I thought . . . they told me . . ." and she rushed to him, threw her arms around his neck, pressed her lips to his and tried to give vent to years of pent-up passion and desire for him. Eventually, Bond had to firmly disentagle himself from his Chief's personal assistant and gently tell her to follow him. "I'll need your help with May, Penny. We've still got to get out of here. There's a fire blazing along the passage, and unless I'm mistaken, quite a number of people who don't really want to see us leave."

He almost dragged her into the passage and pointed her towards May's cell. "Be calm," he said, "and for God's sake, don't show any signs of panic. Just get May out here as quickly as you can, then do as I tell you."

As soon as he saw her respond, he ran through the thickening smoke, toward the elevator doors. *Never use elevators in the event of fire.* How many times had he seen that warning in hotels? Yet, now, there was no alternative. Like it or not, there appeared to be no way out of the passage but by the elevator.

He got to the curved steel doors and jabbed at the button, knowing there was always the possibility that others were making their escape—from the floors above—by the same method; or that the mechanism had already been damaged. His hearing was gradually getting back to normal, making him aware of the roaring of fire from along the passage—from behind the doors of the execution chamber.

290

Reaching out, Bond touched the curved metal doors and found them distinctly warm. He waited, jabbing again at the button, then checking the Uzi and the automatic pistol, which turned out to be a big Stetchkin, which meant a twenty-round magazine, if full, and he had only loosed off six shots. The Uzi would by now be almost empty, so he switched it under his left arm, holding the Stetchkin in readiness.

Moneypenny came slowly along the passage, supporting May, just as the elevator doors opened to reveal four men, in dark combat jackets. Bond took in the surprised looks and the slight movement as one of them began to reach toward a holster at his hip.

Bond's thumb flicked on the Stetchkin, clicking it from single shot to automatic, and turned his hand sideways—for the Stetchkin has a habit of pulling violently upward on automatic fire. If turned sideways it will neatly stitch bullets from left to right. The burst fired by Bond was a controlled six rounds, and when it was over, the four SPECTRE men were littering the floor of the elevator, leaking blood badly over the carpeting.

He held up a hand to stop Moneypenny bringing May any closer while he quickly hauled the bodies out of the cage with little ceremony, jamming one of them across the doors to keep them from closing.

The whole episode took less than thirty seconds, and when it was done he ushered the two ladies toward the lift, which was rapidly becoming very hot.

291

Pulling the body out, and stepping inside, Bond pressed the *Down* button, keeping his finger on it for five or six seconds.

When the doors next opened, they were facing the first curved passage along which Nannie had taken him from Tamil Rahani's room.

"Slowly," he cautioned May and Moneypenny. "Take care." As though in answer to his warning a burst of machine-gun fire rattled in the distance— from along the passage, toward the room originally occupied by Rahani.

It crossed Bond's mind that something odd was now going on. A fire was obviously blazing above them, yet they would be the only valid targets for any SPECTRE people active on the island. Why, then— he asked himself as he moved, close to the wall, along the passage—was there any shooting going on that was not directed at them?

The door to Rahani's room was open, and as Bond reached it, there was a violent burst of fire from within. Slowly he edged into the doorway. Two men—dressed in dark combat jackets similar to those worn by the men in the elevator—manned a heavy machine gun, set up near the big sliding windows. They were firing down into the gardens, and beyond them Bond could see a mass of activity—helicopters, their lights blinking red and green, hovered around the island, a star shell burst high in the velvet night sky, and three sharp cracks, followed by splintering glass, left him in no doubt that the house was being fired at.

He only hoped that the men out there were on the side of the angels as he stepped into the room and placed four bullets neatly into the necks of the two machine-gunners.

"Stay in the passage! Stay down!" he shouted back to May and Moneypenny.

There was a second's silence, and then he heard the unmistakable sound of boots clanking up the metal steps leading to the terraced balcony outside the window. Holding the pistol low, he now called in the direction of the window, "Hold your fire! Escaping hostages!"

The next thing he saw was the burly form of a United States Navy officer, brandishing what looked like a very large revolver. He was followed by half a dozen naval ratings, armed to the teeth, and behind them the white, frightened face of Sukie Tempesta, who cried out, "It's them. It's Mr. Bond and the people they were holding to ransom!"

"Bond?" Snapped the naval officer.

"Bond, yes. James Bond." He nodded.

"Thank heaven for that. Thought you were a goner. Would've been but for this pretty little lady here. Best get out fast. This place'll go up like a fired barn in no time." He was a leathery-faced man, with what used to be called gimlet eyes back in the days when a gimlet was a tool and not just another drink.

He reached out, grasped Bond's wrist and propelled him toward the balcony, while three of his sailors hurried forward to help May and Moneypenny.

"Oh, James! James, it's so good to see you." He had been thrown almost straight into the Principessa Sukie Tempesta's arms, and for the second time in a matter of minutes, Bond found himself being kissed with an almost wild, skidding passion. This time he was in no hurry to break away.

"But what happened? How come the Navy—and, I gather, the Coast Guard—got into the act?" Bond asked.

They had been hurried through the gardens, along paths to the small pier and into a Coast Guard cutter. Now, as it drew away, they all looked back at the island. Other launches and cutters were circling, as were more helicopters, rattling their way around and keeping station with one another, some shining spotlights down into the beautifully laid-out gardens.

"It's a long story, James." Sukie looked at him, eyes doing a very sensual foxtrot.

"Jesus!" muttered one of the Coast Guard officers, and Bond turned to look back. The great modernistic pyramid that had been SPECTRE's headquarters was spouting flame like an erupting volcano, the flames growing higher and higher, exiting through the top of the structure.

The helicopters had started to turn away, one making a low pass over the cutter. May and Moneypenny sat in the bow, being tended by a naval doctor. In the weird light from the Shark Island fire they both looked feverish and ill.

Bond took one more look back.

"She'll blow any minute," the Coast Guard officer muttered and, almost as he said it, the building appeared to rise out of the island and hover for a second, surrounded by a sheet of dancing flame. Then it exploded in a flash of such dazzling violence that Bond had to turn his head away.

When he looked again, the air seemed to be filled with burning fragments and a pall of smoke hung across the little hump that had been Shark Island. He wondered if that was really the end of his old, old enemy, SPECTRE, or whether it would rise, like some ungodly phoenix, from the ashes of the death and destruction he, James Bond, had caused.

— 20 —

Cheers and Applause

SUKIE TOLD HER STORY once the cutter was inside the reef, and the noise of waves, wind and engines grew less, so that she did not have to shout.

"At first I couldn't believe my eyes. Then, when Nannie made the telephone call, I knew," she said.

"Just take it a step at a time," Bond was still shouting, as the ringing had not completely gone from his ears.

When Sukie and Nannie had left Bond on the previous night, Nannie had ordered coffee from room service. "It arrived, and I left her to pour it," Sukie told him. She had gone into the bathroom, to touch up her face, but left the door open, and through the mirror saw Nannie doctoring her coffee, from a bottle. "I couldn't believe she was really up to no good, in fact I nearly taxed her about it. Then

296

thought better—thank heaven. One thing, I re-member, was that I reckoned she could be trying to do me a good turn and keep me out of danger. I've always trusted her—my closest friend since school days. I never suspected there was anything like . . . well . . . She *was* a very faithful friend, you know, James. Right up to this."

"Never trust a faithful friend," Bond smiled wryly. "It always leads to tears before bedtime."

Sukie had dumped the coffee and feigned sleep. "She stood over me for a long time, lifted my eyelids and all that sort of thing."

But, in the end, Nannie had been satisfied that Sukie was out for the count. "She used the telephone in the room," she continued. "I don't know whom she spoke with, but it was quite clear what she was up to. She said she would go down and keep you under surveillance. She thought you might try to make it to the island without us. 'I've got him, though,' she said. 'Tell the colonel I've got him.'"

Sukie had stayed put for a while, "In case she came back—which she did, and made another call. Very fast. She said you'd gone in the hotel motorboat and that she was following. Told them to keep a watch for you, but that you were her prisoner and she didn't want anyone to take you before she did. She kept saying she'd get you to the colonel in one piece. He could divide you. That make sense?"

"Oh, a great deal of sense." Bond thought of the

guillotine blade smashing down and removing Nannie Norrich's arms. "Terrible," he said, almost to himself. "Really terrible. I quite liked her."

"So I heard," Sukie sounded well and truly piqued, and at that moment, the cutter entered the small naval base harbor.

*   *   *

"AND WHO'S PAYING for all this luxury? That's what I want to know." May was obviously well recovered.

"The government," Bond smiled at her. "And if they don't, then I shall."

"Well, it's a wicked waste of good money, keeping us all here in this verra expensive hotel. Ye ken how much it's costing here, Mr. James?"

"I ken very well, May, and you're not to worry your head about it. We'll all be home soon enough, and this'll seem like a dream. Just enjoy it, and enjoy the sunset. You've never seen a Key West sunset, and it's truly one of God's miracles."

"Och, I've seen sunsets in the Highlands, laddie. That's good enough for me." Then she appeared to soften. "It's guy kind of you, though, Mr. James, for getting me fit and well once more. I'll say that. But, oh, I'm longing for ma kitchen again, and looking after you."

It was two days after what the local newspaper was calling "the incident on Shark Island," and they had all been released as fit from the naval hospital that afternoon. Now, May sat, with Sukie and Bond, on the deck in front of the Havana Docks Bar at the Pier House Hotel. The sun was just starting its nightly show and the place was crowded. As was usual, Sukie and Bond ate the huge, succulent shrimp with little bowls of spicy sauce and drank calypso daiquiris. May spurned both, making do with a glass of milk, about which she loudly expressed her hope that it was fresh.

"Lord, this really is the place where time stood still." Sukie leaned over and kissed Bond lightly on the cheek. "I went into a shop on Front Street this afternoon and met a girl who came here for two weeks. That was nine years ago."

"I believe that is the effect it has on some people." Bond gazed out to sea, thinking it was the last place he wanted to stay for nine years. Too many memories were crowded in here—Nannie, the nice girl who had turned out to be a wanton and ruthless killer; Tamil Rahani, whom he had really met for the last time; SPECTRE, that dishonorable society, willing even to cheat others of promised prizes for Bond's head.

"Penny for them?" Sukie asked.

"Just thinking that I wouldn't like to stay here forever, but I wouldn't mind a week or two—perhaps to get to know you better."

She smiled. "I had the same thought. That's why I arranged for your things to be brought up to my suite, dear James." The smile turned into a grin.

"You did what?" Bond's jaw dropped.

299

"You heard, darling. We've got a lot of time to make up."

Bond gave her a long, warm look and watched the sky turn to blood as the sun dropped behind the islands. Then he glanced toward the doors of the bar to see the ever-faithful Moneypenny striding in their direction and beckoning to him.

He excused himself and went over to her. "Signal from M," she said, shooting a few eye-propelled daggers in Sukie's direction.

"Ah." Bond waited.

"Return soonest. Well done. M," Moneypenny intoned.

"You want to return home soonest?" he asked.

She nodded, a little sadly, and said that she could understand why Bond might not wish to leave just yet.

"You could, perhaps, take May back," he suggested.

"I booked the flight as soon as the signal came in. We leave tomorrow." Efficient as ever.

"All of us?"

"No, James. I realized that I would never be able to thank you as I'd like to—for saving my life, I mean . . ."

"Oh, Penny, you mustn't . . ."

She put a hand up to silence him. "No, James. I've booked a flight for May and myself. I've also sent a signal."

300

"Yes?"

"Returning immediately, but 007 still requires remedial treatment that will take about three weeks."

"Three weeks should do just nicely."

"I thought so," and she turned, walking slowly back into the hotel.

"You actually had my stuff moved into your suite, you hussy?" Bond asked, once he had returned to Sukie.

"Everything you bought this afternoon—including the suitcase."

"But," Bond smiled. "How can we? I mean, you're a Principessa—a Princess. It wouldn't be right."

"Oh, we could call the book something like *The Princess and the Pauper*." She grinned again—wickedly, with a dash of sensuality.

"I'm not a pauper, though," said Bond, feigning huffiness.

"The prices here could fix that," Sukie laughed, and at that moment the air and sky around them turned crimson as sun took its dive for the day.

From Mallory Square, where crowds always watched the sunset, one could hear the cheers and applause.